MW00461688

THE GREEN RUSH

LIBBY HOWARD

LIBBY HOWARD
WHODUNNITS WITH HEART

Author's Note:

Although Virginia has decriminalized the possession of personal-use quantities of marijuana and is working toward licensing for production and distribution, at the time of my publishing this book they are not at the stage I've portrayed in the story. I used Maryland and other states to base the legalities and inspection process on, and acknowledge that Virginia's might not be the same once they implement their process and procedures.

CHAPTER 1

"Get in!" Lottie shouted, barely slowing her BMW beside me.

I flung open the back door, shoved Elvis into the backseat, and had my rear barely in the passenger seat before she accelerated.

"What happened?" I asked, shutting my door as we were driving.

All sorts of emergencies were running through my head. My mom was eighty-five and I lived in fear of "that call." Plus, I owned a campground and there were plenty of disasters that might require Lottie to retrieve me while I was enjoying a stroll through downtown Reckless. Although why someone couldn't have just called my cell phone so I could drive back myself, I didn't know.

Instead of turning onto the winding road to the mountains and the campground or heading in the direction of Derwood and the hospital, Lottie swung the BMW down a residential side street and parked.

A crowd was gathered in front of a house, everyone

1

looking up to the porch roof where a woman and a pig were precariously perched.

"The emergency is a pig rescue?" I asked Lottie.

"Pig rescue is a big deal in a town the size of Reckless." She grabbed her purse and opened the car door. "Come on. We don't want to miss all of the fun."

"Fun for whom?" I muttered, getting out of the car and opening the back door for Elvis. "Certainly not the woman or the pig on the porch roof."

Elvis slid out of the backseat. The bloodhound yawned, looked up at the woman and pig on the porch roof, then dropped his nose to the ground to do what he did best—sniff. Drama didn't interest Elvis unless it came with something pungent enough to engage his sniffer.

I'll admit I was just as curious as the onlookers, even if my dog wasn't. About eight people were clustered around the sidewalk and yard of the house, with a couple more jogging up the street, as eager as Lottie to watch the happenings. They were all gathered in front of a cute bungalow-style home sided with cedar shakes. The porch spanned the entire front of the house, and although it looked to be in good repair, I was uncertain about its ability to support a rather curvy middle-aged woman and a pig.

"Is that Squeakers?" I asked Lottie, unsure if more than one person in town had a pet pig. Celeste Crenshaw and Squeakers were town icons and I'd seen him a few times at the Bait and Beer, but I didn't trust my ability to tell one pig from another.

"Oh, yes. It's Squeakers, all right. Although I'm not sure what he, or Celeste, are doing on their porch roof."

Lottie speed walked her way up to the lawn, squeezing between Bart and Bernie Wilson to get a better vantage point. I followed at a more sedate pace, Elvis smelling the ground as he walked at my side.

"Celeste tried to lock Squeakers in so he wouldn't be spending all day at the Bait and Beer," Bart, the younger of the two men, told Lottie and me.

"It's checkers day," Bernie added with a sad shake of his head. "Squeakers loves checkers. Guess he didn't want to miss the game and pulled a jail break."

Nobody seemed to mind Squeakers hanging out at the Bait and Beer with the handful of men who played games on top of a pickle barrel all day and, from what I could see, never bought anything. Only Celeste Crenshaw minded. She went into a panic every time her pig went missing, and instead of checking the one place he always headed to, she went on the Reckless Neighbors app with frantic pleas for someone to find her pig.

"Why didn't Squeakers just unlock the door, like he did last time?" Lottie asked.

"Celeste put on some fancy pig-proof locks. On both doors. *And* on the downstairs windows." Bernie looked up at the pig. "Guess she needs to lock the upstairs windows as well."

"Her plan seems to have worked pretty well even without locks on the upstairs windows," Lottie pointed out. "Squeakers is still here and not playing checkers at the Bait and Beer."

"He's here on the *roof*," I reminded her. "Not safe in the house or safe at the Bait and Beer. How the heck is he going to get down without breaking a leg? Did someone call the fire department?"

I assumed the fire department would be the appropriate emergency service for helping get a woman and a pig off their porch roof. They helped get cats out of trees—at least I thought they did. Maybe that was just an urban legend.

"The fire department's responding to a backyard burn that got a little out of control," Bart said. "We've only got the

3

one truck and three volunteers at the fire department, so Shelly had to send the cops over instead."

Reckless was a town of roughly nine hundred residents, and I wasn't sure if that was counting Celeste Crenshaw's pig or not. Their paramedic was also the coroner. The sheriff and his one full-time and one on-call deputies handled town policing as well as law enforcement for the county. I could see where a backyard fire would take priority over a woman and a pig on a reasonably sturdy roof.

I wasn't sure what the cops could do, or if the plan was to wait for the fire department to finish up with the backyard burn and make their way over here, but I was intrigued by the drama, and not about to leave until the pig was off the roof.

So we all stood there, staring up at Celeste and Squeakers. Waiting.

"How's the wedding planning going?" I asked Lottie to break the silence. Her daughter, Amanda, was newly engaged and my friend had been helping with the arrangements— well, any help that Amanda would allow.

"We've narrowed the dress choices from eight down to three," Lottie announced.

That *was* progress. Lottie pulled up some pictures on her cell phone and showed me the top choices. Bart and Bernie Wilson moved in close, looking at the pictures over our shoulders.

"Sweetheart necklines are a bit dated," Bart mentioned. "I like the lace one if she can get it with a scoop neck."

"I've never been a fan of the form-fitting wedding dresses," Bernie chimed in. "Or the whole Southern Belle look. A-line or fit-and-flare? Now *that's* classic. Gone-With-The-Wind, or Pole-Dancer? That's a no-go."

"Better than those shoulder pads and puffy cap sleeves that were all the rage decades ago," Bart told his brother.

"Peplum skirts." Bernie rolled his eyes. "As if a girl ever really wants her butt to look bigger than it's normal size."

"Some women who are lacking in that area might appreciate the added volume a peplum brings," I told the pair, although I secretly agreed about the shoulder pads and puffy cap sleeves. "Ultimately a woman gets to pick whatever fashion faux pas she wants in her wedding dress, whether that's a hoop skirt or head-to-toe Spanx for a form-fitting dress."

"I love a good peplum," Lottie said. "That little butt-ruffle always looked cute, in my opinion. Not that I need any extra attention there, but I like them. The trend kinda reminded me of a smaller version of the Gibson Girl look."

"Bustle and a big hat," I said. "You should definitely suggest that to Amanda."

"Oh no. We're finally down to three dresses after having tried on an entire warehouse full of options. I have no desire to go back to more choices. She'd better pick one of these, or I'm going to need to resort to pharmaceuticals just to get through the planning part of this wedding."

Lottie had just stuffed her phone back in her purse when the two deputies came around the side of the house. Deputy Sean Cork was carrying an extension ladder. Jake Bailey, our "sometimes deputy" and my neighbor, was carrying nothing. Catching sight of us, he detoured in our direction, leaving Sean to set up the ladder against the porch roof by himself.

Elvis actually picked his nose up off the ground at Jake's arrival, wagging his tail and shoving his head against the sometimes-deputy's leg. Jake reached down to scratch Elvis behind the ears in response to the hound's greeting.

"Sean draw the short straw?" Bart asked Jake.

"For once. Usually I'm the one with the ladder while Sean stands back and shouts helpful pointers and encouragement,"

Jake told us before turning to the other deputy. "Scoot it over about three feet, Sean. That way you won't dent the gutter."

"That there's a very helpful pointer," Bernie commented with a grin. "'Bout time Sean did some work around here."

"Sean does plenty of work," Bart corrected his brother. "It's Oliver who's always slacking off. That man needs to put down his steak knife and actually show up at a crime scene."

Not that this was a crime scene, but I agreed. I hadn't been here long enough to feel comfortable criticizing the local sheriff, though, so I just kept my comments to myself.

We stood and watched as Sean held the ladder steady and tried to convince Celeste to come down. She refused, insisting that Squeakers needed to be saved first. Finally, Sean climbed halfway up the ladder and continued his attempts to persuade her.

"Why don't they just go back in the second-floor window?" I asked. "Evidently that's how Squeakers got out, and I'm assuming Celeste as well since there was no sign of a ladder until Sean brought one around."

"We tried that when we first got here." Jake pointed upward. "See the roof pitch? Squeakers can't get back up there without his hooves sliding. Sean called to him through the window. Squeakers was game once he realized Sean had some watermelon as a bribe, but he slid and came close to falling off the roof, almost taking Celeste along with him."

"And Celeste won't go back inside the house without Squeakers?" I asked.

"Nope. And it's looking like she won't come down the ladder without Squeakers either." Jake cupped his mouth and turned again to Sean. "Grab the watermelon. You'll need to get the pig to come down the ladder first."

Sean shot him an incredulous look. "No way. Can pigs climb down ladders?"

Jake snorted. "Don't be ridiculous. You're gonna need to assist him down."

"That pig's gotta weigh two-fifty at the least," Lottie commented. "I don't want to disparage Sean's physical fitness, but can he carry a two-hundred-and-fifty-pound pig down a ladder?"

"Maybe we should wait for the fire department to finish with the backyard burn fire," I suggested.

"Or call someone with a cherry picker to hoist the pig off the roof and lower him down," Lottie agreed.

Jake shook his head. "There's a heavy equipment company in Derwood, but they can't get anything here in under three hours. We've got Danielle Pouliette and her tractor with the bucket on the way."

Bernie snorted. "Danielle Pouliette's tractor won't go faster than ten miles an hour. By the time she drives it here from her farm it'll be after dark."

"Waiting for the tractor, or the fire department, or the equipment company sounds better than Sean breaking his back trying to carry a pig down a ladder," I countered.

Squeakers looked like he agreed. The pig plopped his butt down on the porch roof and refused to budge, no matter how much Sean cajoled. Finally, the deputy climbed down the ladder and went inside, remerging with a huge water-melon slice.

Climbing back up the ladder, Sean waved the watermelon at the pig, dripping juice all over his hands and the porch roof.

That was when I heard the unmistakable rattle and roar of farm equipment. It seemed that Danielle Pouliette's tractor did go faster than ten miles per hour after all. Good thing, because the watermelon bribe wasn't convincing Squeakers to take his chances on the ladder.

The noise increased and a large tractor rounded the

corner, bucket raised high. I was amazed the driver could see where she was going, since the bucket looked like it was blocking her view, but the driver deftly swerved around parked cars and maneuvered the tractor down the residential street. It came to a stop in front of the house, leaving two long streaks of brown down the asphalt in its wake, thanks to the thick red clay mud coating the tire treads.

A tanned woman in her late twenties jumped off the tractor, her dark curls escaping from a blue bandana. Her worn overalls and heavy work boots were at odds with her very feminine form and the bright red tint that accented her smiling lips.

"Someone needs to move this Kia before I have to drive over it," she announced. As one of the onlookers ran for her car, Danielle looked toward the porch roof, shading her eyes with a long-fingered hand. "Squeakers! Dude! What are you doing up there? Let's get you down before you fall and break your snout."

The pig stood at her voice, grunted, and wiggled his curl of a tail.

"Thank the Lord you're here, Danielle," Sean said as he came down the ladder, still gripping the watermelon slice. "I thought I was going to have to carry a squealing, struggling pig down this ladder."

Danielle's smile broadened. "Glad I can help. Now Squeakers can ride down in style, can't you boy? And Celeste as well."

"I'm not getting lowered off this roof in a filthy bucket," Celeste shouted. "Just get Squeakers safely on the ground, and I'll climb down the ladder."

Danielle glanced at her tractor. "It's not filthy. I haven't used the bucket since I turned the manure pit two weeks ago and I sprayed it down right after."

Celeste winced at the mention of a manure pit. "Thanks,

but I'll use the ladder."

"Suit yourself." Danielle shrugged and headed back to her tractor.

With the Kia moved, she drove up over the curb and across Celeste's lawn. I was the one wincing this time as I saw the huge ruts the tires made in the grass. Although a cherry picker or the fire truck probably wouldn't have done the lawn any favors either. With the tractor in place, Danielle raised the bucket until it overlapped the edge of the roof, lowering it expertly so barely an inch remained between the metal and the shingles.

"Hop in Squeakers," she shouted.

The pig tentatively walked toward the bucket, sniffed the edge before jumping in. The crowd cheered, and Danielle angled the bucket to cradle Squeakers as she backed the tractor and began to slowly lower the bucket.

The bucket was seven feet from the ground, when the tractor made a horrible grinding noise. A backfire and black smoke belching out of the exhaust pipe had everyone retreating. With a shudder the tractor engine shut off, leaving us all to rub our ears, the silence a shock after the noise of the machine.

The silence ended with a loud squeal and the scrabbling of a pig trapped in a metal bucket seven feet above the ground.

"Squeakers!" Celeste Crenshaw scooted across the porch roof and down the ladder, treating everyone to a view of her hot pink lace panties in the process. I was betting she hadn't realized she'd be out on the roof of her porch with her pig when she decided to wear a dress today.

Or maybe she had. Some people had an exhibitionist streak, and for all I knew, Celeste was one of them.

"Seven foot's better than ten," Bart commented. "Maybe the pig can jump."

"That's kinda far for a pig," his brother countered. "I could see it if he was one of those military dogs, but a pig?"

The crowd shifted from staring up at the porch roof to staring up at the bucket. Sean grabbed the ladder and hauled it over, adjusting and repositioning it while Danielle tried unsuccessfully to get the tractor to start.

A snout appeared over the edge of the bucket. The crowd began to shout conflicting advice to the pig about whether he should leap or not. Sean moved the ladder aside, realizing it wasn't a viable rescue option, and scratched his head.

"What now?" I asked Jake, suspecting he was the only one here who might have any ideas on how to get the pig out of the bucket.

"Get some cushions and a tall table," Jake called out to Sean. "If Squeakers can jump a few feet down onto the table, then another couple feet onto some cushions, he should be okay."

The onlookers sprang into action, some pulling cushions off the patio furniture while others went into the house for a table sturdy enough to hold Squeakers. Sean and Celeste remained by the bucket, trying to calm the panicked pig. Soon there was a six foot area padded with brightly colored cushions.

"We can't get it through the door," a man called out. I turned to see four people trying to wedge Celeste's round oak dining table out the narrow doorway.

Jake rolled his eyes. "Then get a smaller table. Or take the legs off that one then put them back on once you get it out the door. And hurry. That pig isn't going to wait forever."

An *oink* and Celeste Crenshaw's impassioned "nooooo" drew everyone's attention back to the bucket where Squeakers had wiggled the front half of his body over the edge. With a squeal, the pig launched himself over the edge and right into the open arms of Deputy Sean Cork.

CHAPTER 2

*S*ean's "serve and protect" instincts were spot on, even if his decision meant he ended up sprawled on a pile of cushions, a two-hundred-and-fifty-pound pig on his chest. Thankfully Squeakers wasn't there long. With a triumphant *oink*, the pig was off the deputy and racing down the street, Celeste after him as fast as her legs could carry her.

"Not like she *has* to run," Lottie commented as we watched the pair turn the corner onto Main Street. "He's just going to the Bait and Beer to catch the end of the checkers game."

"Maybe Celeste wants to catch the end of the game as well," I joked.

We turned around to see Jake helping Sean to his feet. The deputy had his hand on Jake's shoulder and was taking shallow breaths.

"You okay, bud?" Jake asked the other man.

"Pig. Knocked wind. Out. Of me," he gasped. "Heavy. Pig. Like a wrecking ball."

"Well, you saved that pig," Jake said, a hint of laughter in his voice. "The mayor should give you a commendation."

Sean punched him in the shoulder, clearly feeling better. "Next time, you get to catch the pig."

"Hopefully there won't be a next time," Jake replied.

With the excitement over, people began to disburse. A few gathered up the patio cushions, returning them to their chairs. Lottie and I walked over to Danielle who had climbed down from the tractor and was standing in front of it, hands on her hips, attempting to scowl it into starting.

"Need a lift home?" Lottie offered. "I don't think Celeste will mind you leaving this in her front yard until you can get it towed to the farm."

"Actually if you don't mind running me home to get my tools, then back here, I should be able to get it started." She turned to grin at us. "It's not my first rodeo with an ornery tractor. And while Celeste might not mind the giant lawn ornament, I doubt her neighbors will feel the same."

"I can do that. I just need to drop Sassy back at her car. Unless you want to come along?" Lottie asked me.

The old Sassy needed to get back to the campground where there were a million things to do, but the new Sassy insisted that this was supposed to be a day off, even if I *had* manned the camp store until nine, and would probably jump back into things the moment I returned. We were on our fifth week of operations since I'd quit my job and sunk my life savings into Reckless Camper Campground. May had arrived with all of its verdant splendor, and with it we were enjoying a full roster of guests—guests who, my mother reminded me, did not need me hovering around them every second of their vacation. I'd insisted Mom take one day a week off and keep to regular work hours, and she had begun to insist the same of me.

Today was Tuesday. My day off. I'd taken Elvis for a short, three-mile hike this morning after manning the camp store, then we'd come into town for a relaxing lunch and a little shopping. The recent excitement with the local celebrity pig, and a short road-trip to Danielle's farm were the perfect activities to round out my day.

"I'd love to come," I told Lottie.

She made the introductions and we piled into her BMW, Danielle riding shotgun with me and Elvis in the back.

"Nice lipstick, by the way," Lottie said to Danielle as we headed out of town. "That fire-engine red is really flattering."

"Thanks. I think I like it better than the dark burgundy I usually wear. Feels more summery." Danielle turned her head and shot me a quick smile. "My Gran always said a woman should never leave the house without lipstick on. I'm about as far from girly as you can get, but it's a piece of advice I always took to heart."

"It does look good on you," I told her. It used to be I felt the same about mascara, but I'd gotten out of the habit of even wearing minimal makeup during my cancer treatment, and hadn't bothered since. Maybe I should start swiping a little mascara on first thing in the morning again. And maybe tinted Chapstick with the SPF sun protection as well. I doubted I could pull off Danielle's red shades, but a coral or soft pink might be nice.

"I'm so glad you bought the old campground, Sassy." Danielle twisted around in her seat to talk to me. "I wasn't the only one worried that some developer would snatch it up, raze the whole place, and put up a bunch of tacky condos. It's getting harder to buy lakefront properties on the deep part of the lake. Everything is either already built on, or part of the park land, or off in the marshy areas."

"I loved coming to this campground when I was a kid," I

told her. "It truly was a stroke of luck that it was for sale just when I was looking for a career change."

"Sassy used to do corporate event planning and trade show marketing," Lottie told the other woman.

"Well, that *is* a major career change," Danielle commented. "Me? I've always been a farmer. My grandparents farmed. My parents farmed. I'll farm until they till me under with the fertilizer."

"Has your land been in the family for that many generations?" I asked her. "Do you currently farm with your parents? Brothers and sisters?"

I'd always wondered how that worked. Did family farms get divided up between siblings, growing smaller with each passing generation? Did the eldest inherit?"

"I'm farming on my grandparents' land, but we have three farms in our family right now," Danielle replied. "Grandad was very frugal and Gran had inherited a nice sum of money when her parents died, so they were able to purchase two other farms back in the sixties and seventies. When my father and Uncle Josh turned twenty-one, each of them were gifted a farm."

"Wow, that's amazing," I commented.

She nodded. "Land prices have really gone up, what with the increase in lake tourism and development in the last ten years. Some of the kids I went to high school with can't even afford to buy a house, and here I am with a farm of my own. Trust me, I know how lucky I am."

"But you said you're farming your grandparents' land," I mused. "So I'm assuming they've passed, or retired and gifted you the farm? Are your parents and Uncle Josh working the other two places?"

"Not exactly." She wrinkled her nose. "Uncle Josh died in an accident ten years ago. Aunt Erin didn't want to try to manage it herself and neither of their kids were interested in farming, so she sold the farm to my father, and is now living in a lovely beach-front condo in Nags Head."

"That's my kind of retirement," Lottie commented. "Although I'm sorry for the loss of her husband."

"Seems like that happens a lot, the children not wanting to continue on with the family farm." I sighed. "I get that kids need to live their own lives—I doubt my son would be interested in running the campground when I pass. I'm glad your parents had the money to be able to buy her out and keep the farm in the family, though."

Danielle nodded. "Trust me, it took pretty much all their savings, but Dad felt it was important to buy the farm. My parents figured my brother and I might both have children eventually and that we should have enough family land to accommodate the grandkids if they wanted to farm as well."

It *was* nice to be able to leave something to your children and grandchildren, or have enough saved up during your lifetime to help them with school and possibly a down payment on a house.

Putting aside our differences after an ugly divorce, Richard and I had covered enough of Colter's college tuition that he'd graduated with only a few thousand in student loans. I'd chipped in to help pay for some of his wedding expenses as well. He and Greg hadn't needed my help when they'd bought their house in Dallas, but with their talk of adoption and the possibility of a future grandbaby, I'd been thinking a lot about inheritance and estates.

But hopefully all of that would be two or three decades away. I might not live to be Mom's age, but I certainly hoped I did.

"Anyway, when Gran passed away five years ago," Danielle continued, "I moved in to help Grandad full-time. He died last year, leaving the farm to me. My brother, Eli, is still at college, but he'll get my Uncle Josh's farm when he graduates next year. Right now Mom and Dad are doing fine, but if they ever get to the point where they can't manage, or they want to park the tractor and call it quits, Eli and I will both work their farm together."

I tried to follow her convoluted trail of inheritance, and gave up with a laugh. "Well, I'm glad both you and your brother are interested in staying with the family business."

Farming was hard work, and each year it seemed that hard work yielded less and less profit. The big money was in the huge corporate factory farms, as developers slowly gobbled up the fields that used to be the backbone of our food industry. Inheriting land helped a young farmer get started, but even with inheritance, and subsidies, I knew that most farmers were a few equipment malfunctions or bad seasons from bankruptcy.

"Like I said, farmer for life." Danielle held up her hand as if making a pledge.

"What exactly do you farm?" I asked, thinking maybe a mix of livestock and crops since she'd mentioned both manure pits and spreading fertilizer in the fields.

Danielle and Lottie exchanged a quick glance, the former tensing slightly at my question.

"Don't worry, I'm not with one of those don't-eat-meat groups," I told her. "I'm all about humane treatment, but I like my steak as well as the next person."

"It's not that." Danielle hesitated. "I just...well, I grow soybeans."

I waited, thinking that surely soybeans couldn't be a controversial crop.

"And I have about ten head of cattle," she continued hesitantly.

"Oh, just tell her," Lottie interrupted. "It's not like everyone isn't going to find out soon enough—if they don't already know."

My eyebrows shot up and I waited, intrigued to hear what Danielle was farming besides soybeans and ten head of cattle. Tigers? Flamingos? Venomous snakes?

"Pot," Danielle admitted with a grimace. "I grow pot."

"It's legal now," Lottie reminded me.

"It's legal to buy from a licensed dispensary, but I didn't realize it was legal to grow it on a large scale. Or even on a small scale," I commented.

Virginia had decriminalized the possession of marijuana a few years ago, but the logistics of supply and distribution had lagged behind the non-criminalization law. You could have and use pot, but not in public places. You could gift it, but not sell it unless you were a licensed entity. You could own up to six pot plants for personal use, but they each had to be registered and tagged. And the labs that extracted the potent chemicals from the leaves were also highly regulated. I was surprised to hear a farmer actually admit to growing it as a crop—especially since I'd thought that was against the law.

"It's only legal to grow it on a commercial scale if you have a license from the state and a valid contract with a licensed manufacturer or distributor," Danielle explained. "The bidding process was brutal, and the hoops I have to jump through to keep the license are ridiculous. Still, it's a hearty, reliable crop and the money is great."

"Pays better than soybeans?" Lottie asked.

Danielle laughed. "*Way* better than soybeans. Although I still intend to keep some other crops in rotation and I'm not giving up my cows."

"How many plants do you have? How did you get the starter plants or seeds or whatever? Does the crop yield the first year?" I peppered her with questions, completely fascinated that I now knew a legitimate pot-grower.

"I grow marijuana plants on sixty acres." Danielle turned

to look at me. "And yes, that's a lot of pot. I've got four different varieties. And I shouldn't be telling you this, but I started growing them all from seed before I was legally able to do so. Winning the contract and the bid with the state was a total chicken-or-the-egg thing. You had to prove that you had the ability to provide the varieties and quantity they wanted within a certain time frame, but you technically weren't supposed to be set up yet to do so. Like we were all going to snap our fingers and have thousands of pot plants magically appear in our field, ready to harvest in the next six months."

"I'm sure you weren't the only one doing stuff on the sly," Lottie told her.

"Oh, I wasn't, but everyone kept their mouths shut. And those who were reviewing the bids thankfully turned a blind eye on their initial reports when it came to how we were planning to get so many plants up and yielding from zero. If I hadn't gotten the contract or won the bid, I would have lost a ton of money." She laughed. "Or gone into the illegal distribution business. Trust me, I would have been tempted."

"Could you have done that?" I asked, intrigued at the prospect.

"Probably not." She snorted. "There's a lot of random aerial surveillance of farms. Even if I'd hidden them in between rows of soybeans, they would have probably caught me. And it would have been a pain in the butt to harvest and sell that quantity of marijuana. Plus, Reckless is a small town. Lottie is right. There are few secrets that stay secret here. I might have been able to get a harvest or two out, but then someone would have found out and blabbed and I would have had the authorities at my door. It's bad enough that I risked losing my grandparents' farm growing the plants before I was authorized to do so. Getting arrested for illegally growing a controlled substance? My parents would never have forgiven me. Nor my brother. And I'm pretty sure Gran and Grandad would have come back from beyond the grave to rake me over the coals. But luckily that isn't an issue. I've got the license and the contract, and I plan on walking the straight and narrow, obeying every one of their ridiculously strict laws. And making bank."

"Sounds like a valid business plan to me," I told her.

We continued to chat about Danielle's farm, my campground, and Celeste's pig until Lottie turned down a narrow gravel lane flanked on either side with four-board fencing that enclosed a soybean field on the right and a cattle pasture on the left. Black and brown cows grazed in the field, oblivious to the BMW passing them by. Elvis perked up, sitting tall in the back seat and sniffing at the crack of the open window. I smiled, wondering if he'd ever been up-close with a cow before.

Danielle's residence was a weathered brick, two story structure that looked like it dated from the late eighteen hundreds. The wraparound porch was lined with mismatched benches and chairs, some plastic cat hutches, various tools, and several pairs of muddy boots. A large orange cat rose from a sunny spot in the yard as we parked, stretching and meandering his way over to greet us. To the left of the house stood several outbuildings. The huge bank barn showed round bales of hay through the open door. An equally large but more modern barn next to it held all sorts of tractor attachments along with an ancient combine. A big chicken coop was closer to the house, the hens free-range and pecking their way around the side yard.

"Feel free to look around and stretch your legs," Danielle said as she hopped out. "I'll just gather my tools together, put them in Lottie's trunk and we'll get going. I don't want to be rude, but I'll need to give you both a rain check on the hospitality until I can get my tractor off of Celeste Crenshaw's front lawn."

"We completely understand," Lottie called out as the woman jogged toward the house.

Elvis and I got out of the backseat of the BMW, taking Danielle up on the offer of leg-stretching. Lottie's BMW was spacious, but the backseat still wasn't all that comfortable for a grown woman and a hundred-pound bloodhound.

"Leave it," I told Elvis as I saw him eyeing the cat. My hound loved felines, but they didn't always return his affection. I didn't want him upsetting one of Danielle's barn cats, so it was best to have him keep his distance from the get-go.

Elvis sighed, then immediately glued his nose to the ground and began sniffing. I watched, amused as he wove a complex path around the front and side yards, ignoring the cat and the chickens as he concentrated on whatever he was smelling. I walked around to the barn with the farming implements, something in a tiny patch of weeds that were growing in the gravel near the door twinkling in the sunlight and catching my eye. I bent down and picked up a broken gold chain with a small heart pendant attached. There were tiny diamond chips along one side of the heart.

Outside of the lipstick, Danielle didn't seem like the sort of woman to wear this kind of jewelry, but the necklace wasn't dirty or half-buried in the gravel, so it had clearly been recently dropped. I pocketed the piece of jewelry, thinking I'd give it to Danielle on our ride back, then continued around behind the house to explore.

Danielle's farm was pretty. I admired the neat vegetable garden behind the chicken coop as well as the fat, friendly hens who came over to see if I had any grain in my pockets to share. The sun was warm, the air cool, and the rolling fields of small green plants picturesque. I left Elvis to his sniffing and walked down to the crop field behind the house, wanting to see marijuana plants live and in the flesh as opposed to what I'd seen in those anti-drug documentaries I'd had to watch in high school.

They were beautiful, bright green and about a foot high, their jagged-edged leaves waving in the faint breeze. The soybean sprouts growing in the field down the drive were smaller and not as pretty, although I really loved the bright gold of a soy field in the fall, just before harvest. I stood there admiring Danielle's farm, marveling at the fact that I was here looking at acres and acres of pot plants, all completely legal. It was surreal given the villainization of the plant as a "gateway drug" and "the devil's lettuce" during my youth.

With a sigh I turned around, calling to Elvis. Danielle was probably done loading her tools in the car and I knew she wanted to get back to her broken tractor. And I needed to get back to the campground as well.

Elvis didn't come. Which wasn't all that much of a surprise. Hounds ranked pretty low on the obedience scale. They were independent and purpose-bred to have unbreakable focus when it came to scent tracking. Normally I kept Elvis either on a leash or on an e-collar where a quick vibration would get his attention and alert him that he needed to return to me. Since we'd been in town shopping, I hadn't put his e-collar on, and when I'd gotten out of the BMW, I'd unsnapped his leash, thinking he'd stay within sight.

I should have known better.

I called him once more as I jogged to the barn, irritated with myself for not keeping an eye on my dog or ensuring he stayed nearby. With so many things to smell, Elvis was probably on his way to the manure pit or the chicken coop right now.

Rounding the corner of the building, I saw my bloodhound, sniffing around the edge of the field of marijuana plants. I called him once more but he ignored me and, to my horror, flattened several plants with a firm stomp of his paw.

Mortified that he was destroying Danielle's valuable crop, I ran for him. That's when I saw that there was something else at the edge of the pot-field. A pair of boots.

And connected to those boots was a body.

CHAPTER 3

The three of us stood next to the dead man in the field of marijuana, waiting for the police to arrive.

After I'd seen the corpse I'd dragged Elvis back to the car, snapping on his leash and telling the others what the hound had found. Then I called 911 as Elvis and I jogged back to the body. Thankfully Lottie's speed walk was just as fast as my jog, because I had no idea what the address to Danielle's farm was.

As Lottie gave Sheila the address and argued with her about the need to actually send someone out to us, I stood vigil over the body with Danielle.

"Do you know him?" I asked, trying to keep Elvis from sniffing the body and further disturbing any evidence.

Danielle shook her head. "I've never seen him before. And where's his car? How'd he get here?"

She'd raised a good point. Lottie's BMW was parked beside a battered, mud-splattered truck that I assumed belonged to Danielle. There was no other car in the driveway or down by the barn, or on the long gravel drive to the house. How *had* the man gotten here?

23

"How far is it from town?" I asked, trying to remember how long we'd been driving to get here.

She snorted. "Too far to walk. Six miles give or take. I had to practically red-line my tractor's engine to get to Celeste's in a reasonable amount of time. I wouldn't want to have to walk that distance. Or run. Especially in *those* clothes."

It was another good point. The guy was wearing a suit, and a pair of nice leather loafers. Not exactly the attire and footwear to walk or run six miles.

"So maybe he parked down the road?" I speculated, thinking that wouldn't be such a long walk, although the driveway was long, and those loafers...

"We would have passed his car on the shoulder unless he pulled into someone's driveway and parked there. Trust me, you don't pull into someone's driveway around here without them knowing about it and coming out to greet you." She stepped closer, leaning in to get a better look at the man's face. "He's not one of the neighbors. And I know most of their kin. Plus, the guy's wearing a suit. Who the heck wears a suit out to a farm?"

Or those shoes.

I thought about it a second then shrugged. "Process servers? People collecting for the Volunteer Fire Department? Jehovah's Witnesses?"

She wrinkled her nose at my suggestions. "If he's one of those door-knocking-for-God people, then where's his Bible?"

I held up my hands. "Whoever killed him stole his Bible?"

"I can't see murdering someone over a Bible," Danielle commented. "Not when the things are in every motel room dresser drawer. Heck, I'd bet any church in town would give you one for free if you asked."

"It could have been a special Bible. Last month someone

was killed over a book with bird illustrations," I told her, thinking of my deceased handyman, Daryl Butts.

"I hope that's not what happened. Killing someone over the Lord's word? What's the world coming to that people would do such a thing?" She leaned in once more. "As far as I know no one's suing me, so that rules out a process server. I don't know what's worse, someone killing a volunteer collecting donations for the fire department, or someone killing an evangelist."

I kept my mouth shut, not wanting to admit I'd occasionally wished some horrible things on the people who knocked on my door to save my soul. Mom and I weren't regular church-goers, but we were Christians and the pair of us usually managed to make our way into the local Methodist church a couple of times around Christmas. But that never seemed to matter to the neatly dressed men who'd interrupted our dinner every few months with pamphlets and offers of prayer.

"I hope it isn't someone who was collecting for the fire department or a man from one of the local churches," I finally said.

Neither of us mentioned the condition of the body. Under other circumstances we probably would have speculated on whether he'd died of a massive heart attack or aneurysm, but the wound on the side of the man's head and the blood soaking the ground and splattering the leaves of the nearby pot plants told of a more violent demise.

The crunch of tires on gravel clued me in that the police had finally arrived. Lottie continued to argue with Shelly even after Jake came around the corner. Stef Ostlund, the county paramedic and coroner, was right behind him.

"Not another one," Stef commented with a cheerful voice. "How many bodies are you planning to find this year, Sassy?

Give me an estimate so I can put in for a budget increase to hire more staff."

This *was* getting ridiculous. Three bodies in less than two months since my arrival in Reckless? I'd gone my whole life without finding a body, and now I'd found three, although technically my mother had discovered the first one.

As much as I hoped this man's death was a horrible freak accident, the first two deaths had been murder, so that's what I was anticipating here as well.

I glanced once more at the head wound and realized there were no rocks nearby that the man could have fallen and hit his head on. But there was no conveniently placed murder weapon either. Perhaps it *had* been an accident?

Jake pulled his notepad and pen out of his back pocket and motioned for me to follow him around the corner of the barn. "I'm assuming you found the body?"

"I did." I tugged on Elvis's leash and followed him. Of course I found the body. Lately it seemed I was always the one who found the body.

"Did you draw the short straw this time?" I asked Jake, wondering why he was here instead of the sheriff or the actual full-time deputy.

"Oliver's otherwise occupied, and I convinced Sean to go to Derwood and get some X-rays. I'm a little worried he might have cracked a rib when Squeakers landed on him." Jake glanced back at me. "So, yeah, guess the short straw goes to me this time."

We paused just on the other side of the barn. "So…tell me what happened?" Jake asked, pen poised over the notepad.

I told him about Lottie giving Danielle a lift to get her tools and me and Elvis tagging along, "We were just walking around while she was loading stuff in the trunk, and there the body was, at the edge of the field. I wouldn't have seen him if Elvis hadn't trampled some of the plants."

He hesitated, looking up at me. "You know what those plants are?"

"Marijuana." I felt my face turn red, as if I were the one growing it. Or smoking it. "Danielle said she has a license and a contract, so it's legal."

I squirmed feeling like I was ratting out a friend. Hopefully Danielle hadn't been lying. But why would she tell me, if her crops *weren't* on the up-and-up? And why have a huge field of pot right out in the open unless she was a legitimate grower? She'd explained what the risks were of breaking the law and how easy it would be for her to get caught if she wasn't licensed. I truly believed this was a legal operation after the conversation Danielle, Lottie, and I had in the car on the way here.

Jake nodded, scribbling a few more things on his notepad. "Not everyone is all that happy about Danielle's change in crops. I just wanted to see what your reaction was."

"Not everyone is happy?" I frowned. "But she has a license."

"Weed might be legal now, but a lot of people still see it as a dangerous drug."

"*Reefer Madness.*" I rolled my eyes. "It was a stupid movie, but we all had to watch similar stuff in school and learn about the Devil's Weed. Ridiculous, if you ask me. Marijuana has a proven medicinal use."

"Alcohol is more dangerous in my opinion," Jake agreed. "But lots of people feel otherwise. There have been petitions. Danielle's had a few instances in the last few weeks of someone trying to kill off her plants and burn her field."

Burn her field? Wouldn't that just get everyone downwind high? It seemed like a stupid thing to do if you were concerned about pot being a dangerous drug. And it seemed ridiculously extreme. Danielle was a farmer. If someone was mad at the whole legalized pot thing, then they should take it up with their elected officials. Organize a petition. Or a protest at the capitol. Not try to burn down an innocent farmer's field.

"Is that who the dead person is?" I wondered. "A protestor, or someone here to vandalize Danielle's crop?"

"Could be," Jake said. "We'll know more once Stef does her thing and I check the body for I.D."

I thought for a second, wondering how exactly the man had died and if Danielle would be a suspect.

"Danielle has an alibi," I offered. "You saw her. She was in town rescuing Celeste Crenshaw's pig. Plus, you have to factor the time it took her to drive the tractor there, and come back with us. The man must have been killed while she was in town."

Although he *could* have been killed before Danielle left. It wasn't like she expected her tractor to break down and that she'd need a ride back home. But if Danielle had killed the man herself, she should have had us just drop her off and go, lessening the chance we'd nose around and see the body before she could better hide it. Plus, it didn't seem very logical for her to murder a man, then just leave him in her field of marijuana to run off and rescue a pig. If I'd murdered someone, I'd claim to be in the middle of time-sensitive farm work, bury the body, *then* take the tractor into town. Also, with the tractor's questionable top speed, it wasn't like anyone expected Danielle to be there right away. She would have had time to use the bucket to dig a shallow grave, and hide the evidence, then drive the tractor into town.

That's what *I'd* do.

Not that I'd ever murder someone. Unless they were hurting Elvis. Or one of my family or friends.

Jake, Elvis, and I walked back to the field where Stef was taking pictures. Little numbered cards were scattered around, and more of the plants were flattened than when

Elvis had stomped over them. Lottie and Danielle stood out of the way, and I took a moment to really look at them.

Lottie seemed fascinated by the whole thing. Danielle's gaze was focused out across the field of green plants, her arms folded across her chest as she hugged herself. When I'd first told them about the body, she'd seemed just as shocked as Lottie had been—as I had been. Surely she wouldn't have encouraged us to roam around if she'd murdered a man and rolled his body just barely inside the field of plants?

The murderer *couldn't* have been her.

I wouldn't blame Danielle for being a little paranoid and maybe trigger happy if people had been trying to napalm her crops, but somehow I just didn't see Danielle capable of murder. Or of being such a good actress that her distress over the incident was so very convincing.

"Danielle, can I have a word with you?" Jake crooked his finger at the woman then motioned to where we'd just been.

Danielle nodded and followed him while I scooted closer to Lottie, making Elvis sit by my side.

"Jake said people have tried to vandalize Danielle's crop," I whispered to Lottie. "Do you think that's what happened here? Someone tried to burn her marijuana plants, and she confronted them and…accidently killed them?"

Lottie shook her head. "I can't see Danielle confronting someone intent on burning her crop, accidentally killing them, then driving off to rescue a pig," Lottie said, echoing my earlier thoughts. "Although I'm not ruling out that the dead man might be one of those anti-drug people. There's a group of them in town and I know a few of the people from Reckless who are involved with the group. It kinda makes sense with his car not being in the driveway, though. If he was going to set fire to her field, he'd hardly just drive up to the front of her house to do it."

"Which means he must have walked a good distance."

In those shoes. And a suit. Who dresses in a suit and leather loafers to burn plants? Possibly this guy, I guess. Maybe he decided to do a little arson on his lunch break from the corporate job.

I looked across the field. "We didn't see any cars parked along the road when we were coming here, and Danielle said it wasn't likely he'd park in a neighbor's lane or drive. What's across there? Maybe that's where his car is."

"Most of Danielle's farm butts up against another field, but that section there touches the park lands as well as a bunch of old hunting acreage." Lottie pointed to a line of trees in the distance. "I guess he *could* have parked back there, then cut across her field. But if he was going to set fire to the plants or poison them, then why not do it from over there? Why cross the entire field to start the vandalism so close to the house where Danielle would quickly notice and be able to stop the fire? Or take the risk that she might see a man in a suit walking across her field and stop him before he even set the fire?"

She was right. "Maybe the wind made this a better starting point? And maybe he saw Danielle leaving with the tractor and knew he had time to get the fire going before she could return?"

Lottie nodded. "Yeah, I could see that. But then who killed him? If he saw Danielle leave, then it clearly wasn't her."

I held up my hands, equally flummoxed by the whole thing. "Maybe a neighboring farmer saw him setting a fire, feared for their own crops, and took action?"

"Then why isn't a portion of the field burned?" Lottie waved a hand at the healthy, green pot plants. "A neighbor wouldn't have seen anything until the smoke was really rolling, and by then this guy would have been long gone and a good acre or two already burned at least."

"True," I agreed. "Do you really think someone trying to vandalize a field of pot would dress like that, though?"

Lottie shrugged. "Some people take their attire seriously. Maybe the dead man isn't one of the anti-drug people after all?"

"Could he be an evangelist?" I asked, thinking back on my earlier conversation with Danielle. "Or someone soliciting donations?"

"Or those people who go door-to-door selling what they claim are high-quality frozen steaks." Lottie scowled. "Newsflash. They're not high-quality. They're tasteless junk. And I know that because evidently I'm a sucker for a man in a suit selling steaks door-to-door."

"I'm sorry you got suckered into the bad-steak scam," I told my friend. "But even if the dead man was seeking donations, selling steaks, or trying to save souls, the question remains—where is his car?"

"The killer stole it," Lottie announced. "That's the only explanation."

But then how did the *killer* get here? Did he have a friend drop him off then leave? Was the murderer not acting alone?

And something else bothered me about that suggestion.

"Carjacking in the middle of farmland is a thing around here?" The idea was bizarre. "I think it would be slim pickings for that sort of criminal in this area. Plus, everyone has guns. I mean *everyone*. Shotguns. Rifles. Pistols. Carjacking in the city is one thing, but here? It's farmer-assisted suicide."

Lottie and I fell silent as Stef moved away from the body and called for Jake. He and Danielle walked back, the woman joining Lottie and me while the sometimes-deputy walked over to chat with the coroner.

"I've always known there a chance I might be arrested for growing pot before I was awarded my contract,"

Danielle commented, "but I never figured I'd be in jail for suspicion of murder."

My eyes widened, and both Lottie and I swiveled our heads to face her.

"Jake's not going to arrest you, is he?" Lottie said, turning to give the sometimes-deputy a narrow-eyed glance. "He's not that stupid."

"He's not stupid at all," I countered. "I can see him wanting to question Danielle down at the station, on the record, but he won't arrest her. She has an alibi."

"Not if Stef says that man died before I would have left for town with the tractor." Danielle swiped a hand across her eyes and steadied her lips. "I haven't been in the fields since around dawn when I checked to see if I needed to run the irrigation system. I spent the morning doing some paper-work, spreading mulch in the gardens, taking care of the chickens, checking my calves, and working on some equip-ment in the barn. I'll be honest, if that man was dead in my field any time past seven this morning, I probably wouldn't have known it."

"But what exactly did he die of?" I squinted, as if I could somehow divine the cause of death from my current loca-tion. "Was he hit in the head with something? Shot in the head?"

"Couldn't have been a gunshot," Lottie said. "Unless he was killed while you were in town. You would have heard a gunshot."

Danielle held up her hands. "Gunshots around here aren't exactly rare. Farmers kill groundhogs, or have to put a cow down, or are having a little bit of target practice out back. Hunting season might be far off, but no one wants their skills to get rusty. I might not have noticed if there'd been a gunshot or two this morning."

"Right here, so close to your house?" I asked her. "I think that might have registered."

"Possibly," she agreed. "But Dick Gaver next door sometimes shoots targets, and it sounds like it's right in my backyard, so I might not have paid attention to a few shots this morning."

"Maybe he was stabbed," Lottie conjectured, craning her neck to better view the crime scene.

"In the head? Plus, there was a lot of blood," I told her. "In my very inexpert opinion, I'd call it a gunshot or a blow to the head, not a stabbing to the head. But clearly, I'm no expert in these things."

"I wonder who killed him?" Danielle shook her head. "Maybe I'll get lucky and the guy just fell, hit his head on a rock or something."

No one was ever that lucky it seemed. I'd hoped the same when I'd found a guest dead on a trail overlook, and it turned out he'd been poisoned. But Danielle's hopeful statement made me think further. In addition to not seeing the man's mode of transportation, there also hadn't been any sign of the murder weapon. Or an instrument for agricultural sabotage. Where were the containers of defoliant? The gallons of gasoline or other accelerant to start the fire? A flame thrower? A bulldozer?

Maybe the man wasn't an anti-drug vigilante after all. But why was he here? How had he arrived? Who killed him and how?

We watched as Jake bent down and searched the dead man's pockets, coming up with a billfold. He looked through it, exchanging a few words with Stef before making his way over to us.

"Do any of you recognize the name Wilber Kendricks?" Jake asked Danielle.

Danielle shook her head. "No. Is he a local? Related to

Marsha Kendricks over at the feed co-op in Derwood maybe?"

"I don't think so," Jake said. "This man is from Roanoke. He has documentation that says he works for the state's Cannabis Control Authority. Evidently Mr. Kendricks is a cannabis inspector."

CHAPTER 4

*R*eckless Camper App:
          Congratulations to Emory Burns on winning the checkers tourney at Bait and Beer today. We're thrilled that Squeakers made a last minute appearance to give his commentary on the nail-biting final round. "Oink!"

We were silent on our drive back to Celeste's house. Jake had not arrested Danielle, but neither had he shed any light on what had killed Wilber Kendricks, or answered any of our other questions—like if this was murder or just some tragic accident. After his consultation with Stef, Jake had given us the all clear to drive Danielle back to retrieve her tractor, asking us to please remain available for further questions.

I peered at Danielle's profile, thinking that the woman looked worried. I completely understood. It wasn't just that a man was found dead on her farm, it was that the dead man was an inspector for the state agency that held her farm's livelihood in their hands. Would she lose her contract over this? Would she be considered a suspect? What would have happened if she hadn't gone into town this afternoon, hopefully providing herself with an alibi for the time of death?

What would have happened if her tractor hadn't broken down, if she'd driven it back to the farm, and hadn't noticed the body until tomorrow, or even later?

After dropping Danielle and her tools off, Lottie took Elvis and me to my SUV, promising to share any information we discovered. I certainly hadn't met everyone in Reckless yet, but of those I had met, Lottie was clearly the woman-in-the-know when it came to town events. She seemed to be connected to everyone, and not at all shy about calling her numerous acquaintances up to grill them about local happenings. In short, Lottie was a gossip. And I was the grateful recipient of any gossip she acquired.

And I cared. I liked Danielle, even though I'd just met her. I didn't want anything bad to happen to her or her farm. I not-so-secretly hoped that this inspector had suffered a tragic accident and that his death wouldn't be ruled a murder. Two murders in the last couple of months was two too many. I really didn't want to add a third to that tally.

Even though speculation about the deceased man was on my mind as I drove home, my thoughts kept wandering to my guests and the various events I'd planned for later this week. As eventful as my day had been, I had a campground to run, and we were all still ironing out the kinks on how to make it all run smoothly.

Pulling down the drive to the campground, I scanned the RV and tent sites, as well as the cabins. I made my way to the camp store that doubled as our office, noting some clouds off to the west and hoping any rain would hold off until later tonight. Parking in the lot, Elvis and I went inside to relive Mom who had been on duty since nine this morning. She seemed fresh and energetic behind the counter, chatting with a couple who'd rented cabin eight and another couple who were in cabin two. Another woman who owned a cute Airstream camper was over by the pastry case, looking at the menu to order breakfast and lunch deliveries from The Coffee Dog.

The pair from cabin eight, Drew and Bree, had mentioned on their reservation that this vacation was in celebration of their fifth anniversary. I'd delivered a bottle of champagne the evening they'd checked in along with a batch of chocolate-covered strawberries that Mom had quickly whipped up for the occasion. Six days into their two-week stay, they'd hiked, fished, kayaked, and gone to visit the bird sanctuary. I eyed their clasped hands, and blinked back some sentimental tears at the sight.

The other couple were about the same age, but hadn't indicated they were celebrating any special occasion. They weren't quite the lovebirds that Drew and Bree were, but Caleb and Courtney still seemed the happy couple. They were also staying for two weeks, and the day after they'd checked-in, Caleb had confessed to me that Courtney had recently lost her brother, and that he hoped this vacation would alleviate some of her grief. She'd definitely seemed quiet and subdued the first few days, but then they'd run into Drew and Bree at the Friday night bonfire and for the first time since they'd arrived, I'd seen Courtney laugh.

The four had quickly become friends, and I often saw them at the campground firepit in the evenings, or cooking dinners together outside of one of their cabins.

The woman with the Airstream was Mickey Marx, and I'd been interested to learn that she lived in the camper full time, moving from campground to campground every month or so. She did some sort of documentation writing for a big, global, technology firm and was a regular here according to the former owner's records.

I was thrilled to have several longer-term guests here at the campground. It reduced the flurry of activity during the turnover days, and I loved getting to know guests better during their extended stays.

Mom glanced over at me and smiled. "Sassy! These guests are asking about the Reckless Riders tours. Maybe you can answer a few questions for them since you're the one who met with the owner?"

Caleb stepped back, hands lifted and a grin on his face. "*Drew and Bree* are asking about the Reckless Riders tours. You're not getting me on a horse in this lifetime. No way."

"*Bree* is asking about Reckless Riders tours," Drew corrected the other man. "I'm not convinced about this whole horse thing either. How about the girls go riding, and you and I'll fish instead?"

"Courtney isn't going to give up her daily small-town, cute-store explorations to get on a horse." Bree ran a hand down her husband's arm, lacing her fingers with his and smiling up at him. "You wouldn't let me go alone, would you? What if I need you to rescue me from a rogue, runaway horse? What if I need my man to *save* me?"

"Hon, if you need rescuing from a runaway horse, I am *so* not your man," Drew retorted. But there was a sparkle in his eye that told me that the fantasy appealed to him. I got the impression he might just be convinced if his wife pushed the issue.

I stepped forward, glancing at the brochures in Bree's hand. "I've never personally been on the tours, but Landon Mills has a wonderful selection of safe horses for all levels of riders. He takes guests up on the trails through a Mountain Laurel grove and along the ridge line overlooking the lake. Everyone enjoys a packed lunch, then they all head down to the marsh sections of the lake where bird watching is at its best. The horses swim through a shallow section of the water then go back on the trails for a beautiful view of the mountains as they head back to the stables."

"Not happening." Caleb shook his head. "Still noping out on any horse stuff."

"I don't know," Courtney spoke up. "I might give up a day of cute-store exploration for this."

I looked over at her, wondering how someone could go to a campground at the edge of a gorgeous lake and a forest with an extensive trail system, and go shopping every day while her husband fished and hiked. But people settled into their relationships and forged them in their own, very personal ways. Maybe this was an opposites attract sort of thing, and this vacation encompassed the best of their diverse interests and hobbies. Maybe this was how she coped with the grief of her brother's death. Maybe she truly loved shopping. Caleb had his outdoor activities, and there were a dozen small towns, and adorable shops for Courtney to discover around the county. Although to look at the woman, she certainly seemed outdoorsy as well, with her sunburnt nose, freckles, and lean, athletic body. But maybe she kept fit in the gym, and the sunburn was from walking along downtown streets and exploring outdoor craft shows.

It was kind of a shame Bree didn't go shopping with her, but it was clear Bree was dedicated to spending every moment of her two weeks' vacation with her husband. Maybe if it hadn't been their anniversary trip, she would have accompanied the other woman on a few shopping excursions. Either way, Courtney seemed happy to go off alone each day, returning in the late afternoon or early evening in time for their group dinners.

"Are you all talking about the guy with the horse tours?" Mickey Marxs' dark braid swung as she turned to look at the two couples. "I did that last year, and it was a total blast. Five stars. Totally recommend. I rode a big gray horse named Peanut who was super sweet. The lunch was good, and the views were amazing. I also recommend the bird sanctuary. I was there today and it was fun."

"We've already been to the bird sanctuary," Bree told her. "It was fun, but I'd really like to do this riding thing."

"Well, I give it two thumbs-up," Mickey replied, holding her two thumbs in the air to reinforce her statement.

The guest's testimonial was timely, but I could tell that the men needed additional convincing.

"It's truly a safe experience," I told them. "Reckless Riders is named that because the town is Reckless, not because the horses are wild or there's anything unsafe about the trip. It's gotten great feedback. Several people have said it was the highlight of their vacation."

Several people meant several reviews. I hadn't owned the campground long enough to hear a whole lot of camper testimony firsthand. I was selling the excursion hard because my guests' incredible experiences while on vacation was kinda my mission. That and I got a commission from Landon Mills for each guest I sent his way. It didn't amount to much, but every little bit mattered when I had a big hole in my living room ceiling that still hadn't been fixed and a long list of improvements I wanted to make to the campground.

Bree sighed. "It sounds so romantic. I've always loved horses."

Her husband still didn't look as enthusiastic about the trip, but he was clearly interested in considering anything his wife found romantic.

"There's nothing more attractive than a man on a horse," I teased Drew.

Jake had horses. He'd been a mounted police officer before his retirement and told me that he'd adopted several former police horses, including one that he'd ridden. I wasn't sure how sound they were, if he rode any of them or if they all just lounged around eating hay and enjoying their retirement, but I made a mental note to ask him.

I suddenly envisioned Jake, on a huge bay horse, controlling crowds during a demonstration, or charging across the Washington Mall in pursuit of a criminal. They should make a movie about that. Cops on horseback. And if the lead was a bearded, fifty-something guy who liked fishing and drove an old pickup, so much the better.

"Come on, Drew. I spent two hours at the bait store yesterday while you picked out lures," Bree said, tucking his arm against her side and turning so her breast brushed against his bicep.

I bit back a smile, thinking that this woman was bringing out the serious ammo here.

"I'm in," Courtney announced. "But only if the men decide to give it a go."

"What? No shopping?" Caleb looked at his wife with mock-surprise. "You've gone out every day of our vacation, but a *horse* is going to convince you to stick around? If I had known that, I would have been dragging you to this ranch all week."

Courtney flushed, her hand creeping to her neck. "I think I'm done shopping. It's time I took more of an interest in hiking, canoeing, and maybe horseback riding."

Caleb grinned. He put an arm around Courtney giving her a quick kiss on the side of her head. "I'm so glad to hear that. I'll do it if you go," he said as he turned to Drew. "If I'm willing to make a fool of myself on a horse, then you should be too."

Bree tucked the brochure into her day pack and batted her eyelashes at her husband. "They're probably just walking on the trail rides, Drew. And there's that grab-handle on the front of the saddle if you need it. It'll be fun!"

Drew sighed. "Okay, but that means tomorrow you're going to spend the day fishing with me."

Bree shrugged. "You fish. I'll sprawl out in the canoe in my bathing suit and catch some sun. How about that?"

Drew looked absolutely onboard with that idea. I hid a grin, thinking the man would be combining some favorite activities—fishing and ogling his wife in a bikini. Win-win.

"How about you?" Caleb turned to his wife. "Will you decorate my fishing boat tomorrow in a bikini, since I agreed to do this horse-thing? I might die, you know. A man deserves to fish with his wife half-naked across from him the day before he gets thrown off a horse and trampled to death."

Courtney rolled her eyes. "Oh, the drama. Yes, I'll fish with you tomorrow, but the bikini only makes an appearance if the temperature is above eighty. Goose bumps aren't sexy, babe. Not sexy at all."

"Let's get your canoes reserved for tomorrow then," Mom said as she pulled out the clipboard with the canoe and kayak rental sheets. "And I'll call Reckless Riders for your Thursday reservations. Should I use the credit cards on file?"

I stood back while Mom handled the transactions, her fingers flying on the keyboard as she typed everything into the accounting system, and went over to where Mickey Marx was filling out her food order on the form.

"I owe you," I whispered.

She chuckled. "Nonsense. I did have a good time last year, and am happy to send additional business Landon's way. He's a good guy."

He was. "Can I sign you up for Thursday as well? Ten percent off on account of your glowing testimonial."

"Oh, I wish." Her smile was rueful. "Sadly this isn't really my vacation. I still have work to do, and unfortunately that work is past deadline. The next two days I'll be locked in my camper with the laptop. Maybe I'll go next week, if I can wrap up this project."

Suddenly the nomadic camper-life wasn't so appealing. Although working from a gorgeous Airstream camper in view of a lake and a forested wilderness was a whole lot better than being stuck in a corporate office downtown.

"Let me know," I told her. "That discount offer still stands."

"Sassy?" Mom called out. "Can you go out and reserve the boats for these guests?"

I took the tags from her, went out and attached them to two of our canoes so Drew and Caleb could easily find them tomorrow. We'd taken to tagging each of the reserved boats, since a few weeks ago there had been some drama over a guest who'd assumed they were just up for grabs. The big red "reserved" tags with the guest's name and cabin or camping spot number on them would hopefully keep that from occurring again.

By the time I'd gone back inside, Mickey had handed in her food order and left, and Mom was finishing up the transactions for the riding excursion. Bree looked ecstatic, her hands clutching the brochures and the receipts. Courtney was smiling, humoring her friend, but clearly interested in the planned outing herself. As she should be. I couldn't imagine the woman would have any store left in the county that she hadn't explored in the last six days.

The men didn't look all that excited. I was pretty sure they were going to be reviewing life insurance plans and wills tonight.

CHAPTER 5

$\mathcal{W}$e watched the couples leave. I could barely wait until the door shut before I turned to Mom. "You would not believe what happened today."

She continued typing the reservations into the computer. "I'm so glad you actually took an entire day off instead of just a few hours like you usually do. I'm assuming you had lunch at the diner? Did you run into Lottie in town? How are the plans for her daughter's wedding going?"

"No. I mean, yes I ran into Lottie, but that's not all that happened. There was a pig on a porch roof, then I found a dead body in a field of pot."

Mom's mouth dropped open. Reaching across the counter she put the back of her hand against my forehead. "You're not feverish. Maybe my hearing's going because I could swear you said there was a pig on a roof and a dead body in a field of pot."

"That's exactly what I said." I went to pour us coffee, then we sat down at the little café table while I told Mom about the pig on the roof.

"Squeakers." Mom shook her head, a smile curving up one corner of her mouth. "I need to hang out at the Bait and Beer just to see how good this pig really is at board games."

Mom had started taking the SUV into town for a few hours every couple of days to explore. She'd joined a knitting group that made hats for newborns and cancer patients as well as for the homeless shelter in Derwood and met with them on Sunday afternoons. She'd also signed up as an alternate for the bridge club, and hoped a spot would open up soon on one of the teams. Lately she'd been trying to get me to leave the campground in Austin's hands Thursday evenings so we could go to the Twelve Gauge for their Trivia Night. I wasn't all that comfortable at the idea of hanging out at the sketchy bar after dark, or leaving my campground in the care of my seventeen-year-old helper during our busy season, so I'd nixed that idea.

But I totally approved of Mom spending her time off hanging out at the Bait and Beer watching board games with Squeakers, though.

"I think Squeakers is more of an observer when it comes to the games," I pointed out. "Although pigs are supposed to be really smart. Maybe he *does* play."

"Celeste needs to lighten up a bit and let that pig have some fun," Mom commented. "He's going to find a way to get out of the house if he has to chew through the drywall to do it. If she wasn't so paranoid about him leaving the house he wouldn't have been on the roof."

I nodded in agreement. "Hopefully Deputy Cork isn't hurt. Jake said he sent Sean to the hospital, just to make sure no ribs were broken."

Mom shook her head. "Poor Sean. And I feel bad for that farmer-woman whose tractor broke down as well. Here she was doing something nice, and it cost her a day of work."

"Which leads to the rest of my story." I told her about tagging along as Lottie gave Danielle a ride home, and about the body in the pot field.

"Any idea who the man was?" Mom asked when I was done.

"Wilber Hendricks. A cannabis inspector for the state."

"Marijuana." Mom shook her head. "That's an unusual crop—especially for this area. I'm sure those contracts are hard to get. Hopefully this won't endanger the woman's business. Was it an accident? A heart attack? A stroke? Was he mauled by a bull?"

Did bulls maul? I thought gore was the correct term for a bull attack, but I wasn't up on livestock facts.

"I don't know. It looked like a head wound, but I didn't see any large rocks or anything nearby. I hope it wasn't murder."

Mom nodded. "Normally I'd assume not, but there does seem to be a lot of murder going on lately."

There did.

"If it was murder, what do you think the motive would be?" Mom asked.

I shrugged. "Jake said that Danielle had been targeted by some people trying to vandalize her marijuana crop lately. Maybe one of them did it, trying to get her contract canceled," I pointed out. "Evidently not everyone in this town, or county, thinks legalizing pot is a good idea. I hate to think someone might have gone to those lengths, though."

"Is there any chance that she killed the man herself?" Mom asked. "Maybe he saw something he wasn't supposed to see—something that would have sent her to jail."

"Then why invite us to wander around while she got her tools together?" I pointed out. "That's taking quite a risk that we'd stumble across her crime—especially since I had Elvis with me."

"Let's say it wasn't premeditated," Mom mused. "Maybe it was an accident, and she panicked. Thought she'd cover it all up later once she got home from helping Squeakers off the roof. A Bloodhound's nose is legendary, but maybe she figured with the chickens, cattle, and pot plants, Elvis would be more interested in other things than a body hidden at the edge of the field."

"True." I frowned. "But Danielle seemed genuinely excited about the contract, and she loves her farm. She went to a lot of trouble to get the business with the state, and she knew all the hoops she'd need to jump through to keep that business. It's a valuable contract. I can't see her doing something illegal on the side when she knew they'd have her farm under a microscope. But maybe the inspector was blackmailing her, wanting a payoff for signing off on his report?"

"That sounds like a decent reason for homicide to me," Mom commented.

I nodded. "True, but I can't imagine Danielle as the killer. She wasn't nervous or anxious at all as we were driving back to her house—well aside from the fact she was a little reluctant to tell me what crop she was growing. And when I found the body, she was genuinely shocked. I don't see her as that good of an actor."

Mom held up her hands. "Who else would profit if Danielle lost her contract? Or if this inspector died? I've always said 'follow the money' and there's your killer."

"Maybe a rival farm who didn't get the contract? Or another contracted farm who could possibly charge more with supply shorter than demand?" I thought for a second. "It doesn't *have* to be a money motive. Like I said, Danielle has had a few instances of sabotage on her farm. Maybe someone from an anti-drug group, or someone who is personally motivated, showed up to burn or poison her crop. The inspector confronted them. They struggled. The inspector was accidentally killed."

Although what happened to the inspector's car? Assuming the potential vandal arrived in their own vehicle, he or she wouldn't be able to drive both away. Unless there were *two* potential vandals...

Or the killer had enough time to dump the inspector's car and come back for their own. But if that were the case, the inspector's car must be somewhere reasonably close. It wouldn't be practical to drive the other car miles away, then spend two hours jogging back to get their own car. Plus, it didn't work with the timeline. Assuming the murder happened when Danielle was in town, the killer would only have an hour or two to get it all done.

If it had been me, I would have just left the inspector's car there. But then Danielle would have quickly discovered the body since she would have immediately started looking for whoever was parked in her driveway. No, moving the car meant the body could possibly be there all night and maybe even through the next day, unnoticed and widening the window of time for the crime—which meant the killer might be able to establish an alibi.

"I could see it being someone from the anti-drug group," Mom agreed. "Although our armchair sleuthing would be a lot more productive if we knew what the cause of death was."

I nodded. "I'm sure Lottie's on that. The man had a head wound and there was a lot of blood, but it *could* end up being accidental. I expect a call from Lottie by tomorrow at the latest though, telling me all the details."

"And in the meantime?" Mom asked me.

I walked to the door and flipped the sign to "Closed" putting the "Be Back at 7" sign up in the window.

"In the meantime, let's eat dinner. Chicken poblano, salad,

and a couple of beers?" I suggested, as if Mom didn't know what I'd put in the slow-cooker early this morning.

She hopped off the stool, untied Elvis's leash, and led the hound through the store. "It's a date."

CHAPTER 6

*R*eckless Camper App:
　　Reckless yard sale on July 5th and 6th. Tables are $25 for both days. Sign up at the Community Center and start gathering your wares!

Love cornhole? I make custom sets with your favorite sports team logos, business logos, and more. Contact Wendy VanDorne for a quote.

I put down my coffee and made a quick note in my phone to contact Wendy about a few cornhole sets for the campground. Len had two horseshoe pits over by the garage, but cornhole was really popular around here, and unlike the horseshoe pits, the boxes and beanbags could be stored in the game room closet when they weren't in use. If Wendy's price was reasonable, I might order one, or possibly two sets.

As for the yard sale... I desperately wanted to get rid of all the books lining one entire room of my house. Plus, all that stuff in the attic. I was going to have to box it up eventually, and this might be the perfect venue to unload it all. But who could I pay to sit at a yard sale table for two days? I certainly wouldn't have the time to do it myself. And worse, what if nothing sold and I had to haul it all back home again?

I set a reminder for next week on both items, and sat back, enjoying the peace and quiet this morning. Our guests usually spent most of Wednesday cramming in all the activities they could in anticipation of Thursday morning checkout, but this frenzied activity didn't spill over into the camp store or the office. By this point guests had purchased most everything they needed for their vacation and were just trying to use up the food and beverages in their coolers and fridges. Boats and excursions had been reserved ahead of time.

It gave me the perfect opportunity to relax and recharge. I relished Wednesday mornings because I knew the storm was coming. Some guests would leave tonight rather than having to break down camp early Thursday morning, so I expected a few checkouts around dinnertime, but aside from that, Wednesday was a day to chill—and to prepare for the rush of Thursday.

Checkout was a swirl of activity. Then there was the frantic cleaning of the cabins, the camper sites, the grills. We had a very narrow window of time for guest turnover, and I didn't want to have to stall an early-arrival—especially if they were towing a large camper or had an RV where it would be inconvenient for them to drive around for a few hours until the official check-in time. I actually looked forward to the early checkouts. It gave me a chance to get a leg up on the cleaning. Last week I'd cleaned two cabins at midnight after the occupants had left, just to get ahead.

This morning I'd gotten to the camp store at five-thirty, a yawning Elvis by my side. After getting the coffee going and feeding the hound, I went over the boat and equipment rentals for the day, then I took Elvis for a quick walk around to check the campground and give him a chance to do his business. And now I was having a cup of coffee, contemplating the beauty of the morning and thinking about cornhole sets and community yard sales.

A white van pulled in a few minutes later, just as I was taking a book out of my bag to read. Usually it was Flora who arrived in the coffee shop's white van with the morning food delivery, but sometimes her mother, Sierra, did the delivery if her daughter had an important test or schoolwork that had kept her up late.

The white van I expected. The BMW that was parking beside it I hadn't.

"Lottie! What are you doing up this early?" I exclaimed.

Then I noticed that the woman coming in the door behind her, a huge box in her arms, was Sierra and not her daughter.

"I'm too old for this," the coffee-shop owner groaned as she put the box on the table. "I was up until two this morning roasting beans. Flora's got a test today, and I wanted her to get enough sleep, so I told her I'd make this morning's delivery."

That's her excuse, but what's Lottie's? I wondered as I turned to my friend. I knew Lottie wasn't a morning person, but she looked fresh and energetic, with her blonde hair in its usual curly mullet and her makeup flawless. She was wearing a colorful, coordinated, pants-and-shirt combo, and I ran a quick hand over my jeans and T-shirt, wondering how she could manage to look so put together at six in the morning.

"Bludgeoning," Lottie announced as she made her way to the coffee urns. "Defensive bruising on his arms and shoulders, but a couple of good whacks to the head is our cause of death."

"What?" Sierra squeaked, turning to Lottie. "Wait. Don't say any more. I've got another box to bring in, then I want to hear this story. Grab me a half-caf with a sugar and a splash of milk."

Lottie poured us all coffees, then relocated a third chair over to the café table. I looked out the window at some guests who were pulling their canoes from the racks, smiling to see Bree and Drew among them. The woman had sweat-pants and a hoodie on, but I was pretty certain there was a bikini underneath it all—and that the bikini would make an appearance once the air was a bit warmer.

Sierra brought in the second box. Lottie waited impatiently as the two of us went over the orders and put the food in the back fridge or behind the counter. After the last murder, I wasn't taking any chances. It might require more work from Mom and me, but I wasn't about to have the campers rooting through the box of bagged food, where someone could slip a little poison into another person's lunch.

When Sierra and I were done, we all sat at the tiny café table, coffees in hand.

"So...bludgeoning? I'm assuming you mean that's the cause of death for the body from yesterday, and not just a random outburst," I teased.

"I mean the body. Although I wouldn't rule out a second bludgeoning at this point. We do seem to be having a lot of murders lately," Lottie commented.

Once more I marveled at Lottie's information network when it came to town gossip. Although I was beginning to think that it wasn't just Lottie who was in-the-know about town happenings. In a small town like Reckless, I doubted there were many secrets, and knew that news spread fast.

"Stef is doing her usual labs and other autopsy stuff, but from what I heard it was pretty obvious that the head injury was the cause of death," Lottie continued.

"This is the guy who was found dead in Danielle's field?"

Sierra asked. "I was told he was a pot inspector. Not that I know what a pot inspection actually involves. Does he check the plants for quality? Type of pot? Makes sure she's not putting in an extra acre for private sale?"

I shrugged, since I probably knew less about marijuana than either Lottie or Sierra.

Lottie sat back in her chair. "They spend most of their time inspecting the dispensaries as well as the labs that are drying the leaves and distilling the drug, but they also do inspections of the growers. Each plant has a RFID tag and the IDs are logged in a database. Inspectors spot-check the tags on random plants using a handheld scanner to make sure they're being tracked. They test for pesticide use, which is prohibited. They also check the plants to make sure there isn't any disease like powdery mildew. If the inspector finds any problems, the grower has ten days to address them and is subject to an additional inspection, or their contract is in jeopardy and they may receive fines or even be brought up on criminal charges."

I stared at my friend. "How the heck do you know all of that?"

"The internet," she announced. "The state has a website with a FAQ page."

"All I know is that it's big money," Sierra said. "Danielle worked hard for that contract, but honestly I was surprised she got it. There are a ton of big business growers that wanted the contract, and I'm pretty sure they were greasing politician hands left and right. For a small-town farmer to get in on this? It's a miracle."

"Maybe they gave preference to local farmers over giving the contracts to out-of-state corporations." As soon as I said it, I knew how ridiculous that sounded. Government always seemed to prefer big corporations over the little guy.

"Either way, I'm sure Danielle is wishing she'd stuck to

soybeans right now," Lottie said. "First she has people trying to burn and poison her crop, and now she's the top suspect in the murder of a man found dead in her field."

"Danielle is the top suspect?" My voice rose. I couldn't believe Jake would seriously consider her a suspect. She'd been rescuing a pig, not home murdering someone. Unless Stef put the time of death earlier, when Danielle would have been home. Then it made sense for her to be a suspect, although it was still a bit of a stretch.

"They found the murder weapon in her barn next to the tractor attachments," Lottie said. "It was a heavy metal rod used for tamping dirt or concrete or something. It had blood on it. Stef's office hasn't confirmed that the blood is the inspector's yet, but the sheriff definitely thinks it's the murder weapon and that Danielle did it."

"I'm so not voting for that man in the election next year," Sierra snapped. "For Pete's sake, Danielle lives on a farm. That blood could be from her taking out a rabid groundhog, or butchering a chicken."

I didn't know much about butchering chickens, but I doubted the process involved using a tamping rod. Still, I understood Sierra's point. There were all sorts of innocent reasons that there could be blood on any number of farming tools at Danielle's.

"Even if the tamping rod was the murder weapon, that doesn't mean it was Danielle," I pointed out. "Someone could have killed the inspector, then planted the thing in Danielle's barn. Or took it from the barn to use, then put it back to make it look like Danielle did it."

"So you think someone is trying to frame her?" Sierra asked.

Lottie shrugged. "It *does* make sense. Those people trying to sabotage her crop would get what they want if she lost her contract."

"Not really," Sierra pointed out. "Isn't that anti-drug group suspected of being involved in the vandalism? Danielle losing her contract would just mean the state would give it to someone else. It wouldn't affect the fact that pot is now legal and that *someone* is going to get a license to grow it."

"True, but I doubt everyone with those anti-drug groups is capable of long-term thinking," Lottie pointed out. "They might have been satisfied just knowing that the pot was being grown elsewhere and not in our neighborhood. Plus, there are others who wanted the contract, and they would benefit if Danielle lost her license. Maybe a rival pot-grower did it."

"But killing an inspector over a marijuana contract?" I shook my head. "That seems like a drastic course of action to take when instead they could just screw up her tracking tags, or put in plants that aren't supposed to be there or even take some away, or infest her crop with some of that powdery mildew stuff. From what Lottie said, this is a highly regulated business. It wouldn't take much to get Danielle's contract pulled, and the bad guy wouldn't have to resort to murder to do it."

"But all those other actions would give Danielle ten days to rectify the issue," Sierra pointed out. "Being arrested for murder? Of an inspector? I wouldn't think there would be a ten-day grace period or a way out of that one."

"What if the murder was a case of mistaken identity?" Lottie mused. "I'm not ruling out the theory that someone is trying to frame Danielle, but that camper who was killed a few weeks back wasn't even the intended victim. What if someone was trying to kill Danielle and murdered the inspector instead?"

Sierra snorted. "I've never seen this pot inspector, but I doubt anyone could mistake a man for Danielle. Admittedly, she's not exactly girly when she's dressed for work, but she's clearly a woman, and a farmer wouldn't be out tending their crops wearing a man's business suit."

"Maybe it was an accident?" I mused. "Or at least, not premeditated murder. There have been people trying to sabotage Danielle's crop. What if the pot inspector showed up and caught one of them? The inspector threatened to call the cops, and the guy hit him over the head and ran for it, thinking he'd only knocked the guy out."

"Pfft." Lottie waved the theory away with a hand. "Then why did the inspector have defensive injuries? And even if this person was doing damage to the crop that required him to be carrying a tamping rod, why take the time to stash it in Danielle's barn if he was just wanting to get out of there before the inspector shook off the blow and came after him? No, if that's the case, then the saboteur *meant* to kill the inspector. And they also wanted to frame Danielle."

"True, but it *might* have been more of a spur-of-the-moment murder, rather than one that was planned and plotted out," Sierra said.

I winced, thinking it was still murder, whether done spur-of-the-moment, or planned. Either way, a man was dead, and Danielle was a suspect.

"If the killer was someone there to vandalize Danielle's crop, then wouldn't we have seen some sort of damage when we showed up?" I asked. "Unless the inspector saw the saboteur before they had a chance to do the damage."

"Was there any sign of a struggle where the inspector's body was found?" Sierra asked. "Bent, broken, and damaged plants? That might tell us whether there was a struggle or if the killer just ambushed the inspector from behind."

"Defensive injuries," Lottie reminded us. "Even if the killer tried to ambush the inspector, he must have heard something, turned around, and at least put his hands up. And from what I saw, the wound was on the side of his head, not on the back."

"Either way I think we should probably take a look at Danielle's field," I told the two women. "I was thinking that the timeline is really tight on this murder. The killer couldn't have driven the inspector's vehicle far and gotten back to their own car in time to be gone before we got there. And maybe they dropped something in their haste to get going."

"Road trip!" Lottie pumped her hands in the air and squirmed in her seat. "When can we go? I'm sure Danielle's awake now. She's a farmer and they get up early."

"But I'm sure the police have already been over the whole farm," Sierra chimed in. "What could we find that they didn't?"

"A lot. The police was just Jake. Sean was at the hospital getting X-rays, and the sheriff was probably out eating a steak somewhere. I'm sure Jake did a good job, but he's one guy." I turned to look at Elvis snoozing beside the counter. "And he didn't have a dog with a great sniffer to help him find tiny clues in a giant field of plants."

CHAPTER 7

*L*ottie drove by to pick Elvis and me up at the campground so Mom could have the SUV if she needed it. Then we swung by and got Sierra before heading out to Danielle's farm. Danielle was on the porch as we pulled in. She was pale aside from her bright red lipstick, twisting her hands together as she approached us.

"I appreciate you all thinking this might help, but I'm not sure there's anything you can do at this point. Jake called in some cops from Derwood, and they spent all evening going through my barn and house. I'm pretty sure if there was something to find, they found it."

"Did they search the field?" Lottie asked.

Danielle nodded. "It's a big farm, and they didn't have enough daylight to go up and down every row, but they searched around where the inspector was and about an acre through the crop. They found his scanner—the one he uses for the plant tags. He must have dropped it when he was attacked."

"So the scanner was near where the body was found?" I asked.

She nodded again. "A few rows over, so I'm guessing it flew out of his hand when he tried to block the blow from the tamping rod. It must have broken his arm. Those things are really heavy."

I shuddered at the thought.

"All they found was the scanner in the field, and the tamping rod with blood on it in my barn," Danielle continued. "It has to be the inspector's blood on the rod. It's got to be the murder weapon. Last time I used that thing was two years ago when I was pouring concrete to replace my mailbox pole after someone ran it over. There wasn't any blood on it then, and there wouldn't be any reason for blood to be on it now unless it's the weapon that killed the inspector."

"I wonder if they've found his car yet?" I asked.

"Not that I know of," Danielle said. "I think that's probably the only reason I'm not down at the station trying to hire a lawyer. I might have had time to kill the inspector before I left in the tractor to go get Squeakers, but I wouldn't have had time to go ditch the man's car, then walk back to the farm. Jake knows I was driving that tractor at top speed to get to Celeste's when I did. There's no way I could have made it go any faster to make up the time difference."

"Thank heaven for that," Sierra said. "Well, Sassy brought her tracking dog with her. Hopefully Elvis will find something the police missed."

I looked down at my hound who was already sniffing the ground. "I figured it was worth a shot, but I don't want any of us getting our hopes up. First, I'm sure the police did a thorough job. Second, Elvis was trained in search-and-rescue, but without an object for him to scent-track from I don't know how well he'll do. For all I know, he could decide to track a bunny, or one of your chickens, or just randomly sniff around."

"Should we start him out at the scene of the crime?" Danielle asked. "That'll at least let us know if the inspector walked a few rows of the field, scanning tags or not. If Elvis tracks him up and down the field, maybe we can figure out how long he was here before he was killed."

"And the window of time for his murder would be from when you left in the tractor, to when we brought you back to the farm?" Lottie asked. "How long was that?"

"About an hour and a half to two hours." Danielle frowned. "But there's a problem with that theory. I didn't see the inspector or his vehicle when I left, but the barn where I park the tractor is over there and I was inside working on the irrigation pumps when I got the call about Squeakers. The inspector might have come, knocked on my door, then just went ahead and got started with the inspection when I didn't answer. I ran out with the tractor so fast, I wouldn't have looked back to notice a car in the driveway or not."

"With all the regulations around these plants, I would think you'd be required to have some sort of locked gates or security cameras or something," I commented.

Danielle flushed. "I am, but the state gave me a few months to put them in. The cameras arrived a few weeks ago, but they take forever to set up. They're supposed to go on the driveway and around the fencing at different intervals as well as on the gate. I only have a handful of them set up so far."

"Do the police know about the cameras?" My voice was high-pitched with excitement. If there were cameras then one of them might have caught an image of the murderer.

"They know." Danielle nodded. "I gave Jake the video for yesterday, but it won't do him any good. The cameras I'd set up in the field were all turned and twisted, so they only got footage of the sky or ground. I'm so sick of people trying to destroy my crop and vandalizing my property. I'd hoped that all would stop with the cameras, but it looks like whoever has it out for me is one step ahead."

"Are the police working on that as well?" Sierra asked Danielle. "I mean, vandalism is no joke, especially when you're a small business owner."

Danielle nodded. "Since I've had more than two occurrences, the sheriff seems to be a bit more interested in the situation. As far as I know there haven't been any arrests, though."

"There's that CAD group in Reckless," Lottie commented. "They were picketing outside the Twelve Gauge last week, and at the church picnic on Easter. They seem non-violent, but they've been circulating flyers against the legalization of marijuana. Maybe one of their members decided to go further than just pamphlets."

"CAD?" I asked.

"Citizens Against Drugs," Sierra told me. "They're also against alcohol, gambling, and Presbyterians."

My mouth dropped open. "What do they have against Presbyterians?"

"Nothing except that the head of CAD, Gwen Sarlet, is also head of the social committee for the Baptist church. She dropped the ball one year and lost the annual Easter Day rental of the park gazebo to the Presbyterian Church, and has blamed them ever since. The Baptist Church is all forgive-and-forget, but Gwen holds a grudge, so she has the CAD group picket every Easter at the gazebo during their service. Petty, but that's life in a small town sometimes."

"I can't see Gwen trying to poison or burn my crop," Danielle said. "She did send me a long, harshly worded letter when I got the contract, saying how my grandparents would have been ashamed to see what had become of their farm, and she does walk the other way when she sees me on the street or in the grocery store. But it's a big step from that to actual vandalism."

"But some of Gwen's followers might be a bit more zealous," Lottie pointed out. "I'm thinking there might be a connection between the group, the vandalism, and the murder."

"I'm sure the police are looking in that direction," Danielle said. "I gave them the note Gwen sent me when I got the contract. If we're connecting those dots, then they probably are as well. Well, at least Jake is. And Sean if he's cleared for active duty after having a pig fall on him. Sheriff Oliver…him I'm not so sure about."

I made a "harrumph" noise. "When is the next election for sheriff?"

"October this year," Lottie replied.

"Please tell me there's someone running against him. Or there's a strong write-in campaign candidate."

Sierra shot me an enigmatic grin. "Maybe we should all write in Jake's name."

I winced, not wanting to be blamed for my neighbor being voted into an office he didn't want—especially when he was supposed to be enjoying his retirement. He'd already gotten roped into this "sometimes deputy" job. Being the county Sheriff probably wasn't something Jake would want at all.

"Well, I know everyone has things to do. Sassy needs to get back to the campground sometime this afternoon, so let's see what Elvis can find," Lottie announced with a clap of her hands.

Elvis had already gotten to work as we'd talked and was over by the barn where Danielle said she stored her tractor. I wanted to set him on a scent track where he'd found the body, but didn't want to discount that he might be tracking the inspector's car, or the murderer, or some important clue, so I jogged over to where he was sniffing, the other women behind me.

Elvis was hot on the scent, his head sweeping back and forth, nose glued to the ground as he made his way around the barn. He jerked to a stop, then bent the front half of his body down to stick his nose under a gap between the barn floor and the ground. I bent down as well, scooting him aside and using my cellphone flashlight app to shine in the space.

"What is it?" Danielle asked, her eyes wide.

"Is it a clue?" Sierra squatted beside me, pulling out her own cell phone.

"Nope." I reached into the space and pulled out...an egg. "There must be a dozen of them in there."

Danielle blew out a breath. "That darned Minerva. I *knew* she wasn't laying in the nesting box. She's going to have to be on house arrest in the coop until she remembers where the eggs are supposed to go."

I put the egg back, figuring Danielle could sort through them later. By the time I'd stood and brushed the dirt off my jeans, Elvis was off again, following another scent. I trailed after him, the ladies behind me in a line as if my hound dog were some sort of canine Pied Piper.

In the next half hour we'd found a pile of deer poop, a very decomposed groundhog, and one of Danielle's barn cats, who was very annoyed at the large, floppy-eared, hound disturbing his slumber.

"Okay, buddy. I don't have time for this," I told Elvis as I snapped on his fifty-foot tracking leash. Balling the excess up in my hands, I pulled him away from what was probably another random scent trail and led him around to the edge of the field where he'd found the inspector yesterday.

"Work." I pointed to the ground and Elvis immediately lowered his head, making loud snuffling noises as he took in the myriad scents. "Find," I told him, not sure what he'd make of that command. When we'd done our search-and-rescue training, I'd always had an item heavily laced with scent for him—usually a sock or an undershirt if we were tracking a person, or a bit of fur or bedding if we were tracking an animal. I assumed that the inspector's would be the predominant odor on the ground, but I didn't fully understand a dog's nose. For all I knew, Elvis might ignore that scent and head off in search of a chicken who'd walked over this patch of land in the last few hours.

But instead of taking us toward the chicken coop, Elvis set off across the crop field. He kept to the space between the plants, which led me to believe that he might actually be on the path the inspector took before his death. An animal would have zig-zagged across the rows, but someone who was being cautious around the crop, someone who was scanning the little tags that were affixed to each plant, would stay carefully in the dirt path between the rows.

We remained in a neat little line until halfway through the field. Then Elvis jumped across the rows, speeding up as he made a diagonal through the plants. I grimaced, hopping over the green leaves and trying my best not to damage any of the valuable crop. From the sounds behind me, Lottie, Sierra, and Danielle were doing the same.

We were about fifty feet from the edge of the field when Elvis hesitated, sniffing the ground before turning back toward the barn in a straight line between the rows.

"Hold up," I told him, shortening the leash. "Elvis, wait. Stop."

It took a few tugs on the leash for him to register what I was saying. Elvis was a good boy, but he was a bloodhound, and they were bred to be independent and focused. When he was on a scent, he didn't seem to register anything else except the odor he was tracking. I swear there could be a tornado, a bomb detonation, and a plate of steak five feet from him, and he'd ignore them all if he was tracking a particularly intriguing smell.

"Why would the inspector have cut across the field like that?" Danielle asked as I gathered Elvis in closer to me and waited for the others to catch up. "I would have expected him to go to the end of the row, then come down another one. I get that the man can't scan every ID chip, and that this should be a random inspection, but it seems like an odd way to go about it."

"I agree." I looked around. "Do you know how those scanners work? Does he have to bend down and hold it to each tag, like when you're scanning bar codes at the supermarket checkout?"

She shook her head. "No, it picks up the signal from the tag while he's standing. All he has to do is walk down the row kinda slow and the scanner will grab the info from the tags. But if he wants to see if I've got any untagged plants, then he needs to take his time and check each one."

"He'd have been here all day if he'd wanted to do that level of inspection." Lottie glanced back at the farmhouse.

"I've only had two inspections, including this one," Danielle told us. "The first one the woman went up and down four rows, scanning tags, then she went back to random areas of the field and actually got down to check the plants. She was here about three hours."

"A woman? You don't always have the same inspector?" I asked, thinking this might be important. Did they rotate? Was the victim just a random inspector out of Roanoke, or someone who was regularly assigned to the area?

Danielle's eyebrows came together. "I think she said something about a new hire or transfer, and her being assigned to a different region going forward. I'm so bad with names and don't remember who she was, but I know she was a woman and that she said to expect someone else next time.

But I think I'm normally supposed to have the same inspector. I assume it's a regional kind of job, like with restaurant health inspections or alcohol inspections in bars?"

"But the first inspector didn't go cutting a diagonal across your field like this?" Sierra waved a hand at the path we'd taken. "It's like this guy saw something that made him head for it, then in this spot right here, he decided to go back."

"Something or someone," I commented. "Danielle, what's on that side of your field?" I pointed to where we would have ended up if we'd continued on the diagonal line.

"Briars and poison ivy?" She laughed. "Seriously, that's about it. There's a few old hunting cabins and the state park. On the other side of the mountain are more farms."

"Is there a road?" I asked.

She shrugged. "Barely a road. It's mud and dirt and not something I'd drive down unless I had four-wheel drive. If it's been raining, I wouldn't head down there without a lifted truck and a winch. Those cabins don't see much activity until fall, so the road, if you can call it that, gets overgrown. Even in the fall, there's not a lot of activity. I think the cabins are owned by people in Roanoke who don't do much hunting anymore. Far as I know those cabins have been handed down for the last four generations. No one sells, but no one seems to use them on the regular either."

"Sounds like the perfect place to sneak onto your farm from," Lottie announced.

"If you don't mind ticks and poison ivy," Danielle countered.

I hesitated at that.

Sierra started walking across the field. "Let's check it out anyway. I don't mind ticks and poison ivy. I'll shower and do a quick check at home before I relieve Mary Alice at the coffee shop."

Danielle grimaced then followed her. "I get poison ivy

just looking at the stuff, so I'm not going to be bushwhacking through the weeds at the end of this field. Just sayin'."

Thankfully I didn't have the farmer's problem with poison ivy. I'd get a red bump or two, and they'd itch, but they never seemed to spread. And if I put hairspray on the bump, it didn't really itch either.

I'd gotten the hairspray idea from my dad. Like Danielle, he'd gotten poison ivy if he was within ten feet of the plants, and suffered horribly. He'd spent his honeymoon covered in itchy red welts because two nights before the wedding, at his and Mom's joint bachelor-and-ette party, he'd gotten tipsy, wandered off, and plopped down in a patch of poison ivy to recite romantic poetry to my mother, who tried in vain to get him upright and back to the party.

My mother still laughed at how they'd spent their wedding night with my dad dotted in pink Calamine lotion. She'd confided that even intense itching hadn't kept him from rocking her world, but that his spotted appearance hadn't really provided the swoon-worthy image she'd imagined for her honeymoon.

After three years of marriage and more than a few occurrences of poison ivy, Dad had stumbled upon relief when in desperation he'd coated his spots with Mom's Aqua Net hair spray. Affectionately known as "hair cement" in our household, the hairspray had done the trick. The alcohol dried the spots, and the lacquer had kept the air from reaching the skin, which relieved the itching. Like that Greek wedding movie with the father who insisted every ailment could be solved by Windex, my father had become a hairspray evangelist.

I was grateful I'd inherited my semi-immunity from my mother, and didn't end up looking as if I had a case of measles every time I brushed against a plant while hiking. I was also grateful for hairspray when I did get a spot or two of poison ivy. My mother's and my days of Aqua Net were over as far as the hairspray's official use. Mom sported a chin-length bob of straight silver hair, soft and product-free. My hair was still in a pixie cut, grown out from the shaved look of someone going through chemotherapy. So any bottles of hairspray in our bathroom cabinet were for medicinal use only at this point.

We reached the edge of the field, and as Danielle had said, it was packed with weeds and briars, along with the tell-tale three-leaved poison ivy on the ground and snaking up the trees. Danielle held back, while Lottie, Sierra, and I carefully picked our way through the weeds toward the road. I wished we'd brought some clippers, or at least leather gloves, because poison ivy aside, the briars looked intimidating.

Elvis didn't care one bit about the thorns or the poison. He plunged into the mess of weeds, and they shook as he snaked his way through it all, snuffling and smelling the scents.

"I haven't put any security cameras out here yet," Danielle called out, waving to where empty brackets stood ready for their installation.

"Is this wire hot?" Sierra asked, pointing to the fencing at the edge of the field. Elvis had blown right through it, but with electrified fencing, it was a roll of the dice whether you'd get zapped or clear the wire before the pulse of electricity gave you a painful shock.

"Yes, but it isn't working right now for some reason," Danielle told us. "I was planning on fixing it today."

Careful not to snag my clothing or skin, Lottie, Sierra, and I wiggled under the fence wires and followed Elvis, even though at this point he could be tracking a rabbit.

We plowed through the overgrown grass, briars, and vines. I tried not to touch anything, glad that I'd worn sturdy pants and a long-sleeve shirt. The long leash I always used on

Elvis when we were tracking pulled tight, and I held him back rather than letting out the slack. We made our way through about fifty yards of overgrown wilderness complete with muddy marshy spots and swarms of bugs until I finally saw the rustic road Danielle had mentioned. Elvis was standing in the middle of the narrow semi-cleared dirt path, waiting for us to catch up. I gathered up his leash as I broke free of the weeds, Sierra and Lottie right behind me. I'd been up front since Elvis was in the lead, and my pants were covered with vegetation and thorns.

"Guys! Look!" Sierra pointed several yards down from us where there was a clear path through the weeds, parallel to the one we'd taken. The weeds were flattened, the briars and branches bent and broken back. I blew out a frustrated breath that we'd forged a trail when we hadn't needed to and walked over to look down the path someone else had recently taken.

And there, a few feet from the rudimentary road, was a red gas can, discarded in the weeds.

CHAPTER 8

here was a possibility that someone who used the hunting cabins, or who had found this road ideal for quick liaisons or an impromptu beer party, had ditched the gas can, but I couldn't see why. No one would have walked down this dirt track with a gas can in hand, just for grins. And people who carried gas cans in their vehicles were probably heading home to mow lawns, or going on trips where they'd need to fuel an ATV or possibly put a little extra into their truck's tank. There certainly could be someone who owned one of the cabins down the road, who needed a gas can to power a generator. But why ditch it on the way out? Why throw a perfectly good gas can away then need to buy a new one the next time?

But if someone had planned to burn a field of pot, and gotten scared off...

"What's going on?" Danielle shouted. Her voice sounded closer than expected and I wondered if curiosity had overcome her desire to stay away from the poison ivy.

I picked up the gas can, noting that it looked fairly new. It was clean of dirt and rain-splatter, and didn't have overgrown weeds holding it fast to the ground. It had been tossed recently—very recently. And there was still some liquid sloshing around in the can. I sniffed the black nozzle, and clearly smelled gasoline.

Had someone come down this road intending to burn Danielle's pot plants, only to be noticed and scared off by the inspector? If so, then they'd clearly run back to the safety of the road and their car, ditching the evidence along the way. But that scenario didn't necessarily mean that person killed the inspector. Someone running away and tossing their gas can in a panic, didn't sound like the sort of person who would then circle around to Danielle's driveway to kill the inspector who'd seen him.

Unless the inspector recognized them, and they were worried about being identified to Danielle or the authorities. Although trespass, even trespass with possible criminal intent, didn't feel like a valid reason to kill someone and risk going to jail for murder. None of the field had been burned or damaged, so all the intruder would be up for was a minor trespass charge, even if the police found and could link the gas can to him or her. Unless there was something going on here that I didn't realize, or a past issue between the inspector and the trespasser that I was unaware of, it didn't make sense.

I put the gas can where I found it, called Elvis back from where he was sniffing a fallen log and returned to the dirt road. It was narrow and overgrown with weeds and briars as Danielle had said. Ruts from years of tire tracks had worn down the outside edges, leaving a hump of dirt and grass in the center. I wouldn't have wanted to bring a car down here, and imagined that even my SUV might get hung up on the uneven road.

"Lottie! Sassy!" Sierra waved from farther down the lane. "Come over here. I've found a car."

Elvis and I jogged down to meet her, Lottie doing her speed walk thing that was just as fast as most people's run. As we approached, I noticed that a six-foot swath had been crushed from a thick section of overgrowth on the opposite side of the road. I drew even with Sierra and saw what she'd seen. Down a ditch with the trunk angled barely above the level of the road was a small black sedan. There was a faint coating of dust and pollen on the shiny surface of the car. The wheels and wheel wells were covered with thick mud, and I could see where the dirt had splattered up along the fenders. In spite of that, this vehicle clearly hadn't been here for long. Like the gas can, it was just too shiny.

Someone might have turned down a wrong road and gone off into a ditch then left, intending to get a tow truck the next day to pull them out. But why not call and get towed right away? Why walk what was probably three miles to the nearest service station when one phone call could bring help? I pulled my cell phone out, noting that I had four bars of service. Why leave the car when help would be a phone call away?

Maybe the driver was drunk and wanted to wait until they sobered up before calling the accident in. Maybe this was a stolen car, and whoever had lifted it had just abandoned it here. Or maybe this was the inspector's car, ditched here after his murder. If we hadn't been nosing around Danielle's field and forging our way through the weeds beyond it, we wouldn't have found this car or the gas can. I doubted anyone would have found it until fall or later, depending on whether any of cabin owners decided to come out and hunt. Possibly it might have remained hidden even then, overgrown by weeds by the time autumn came around.

"I'm calling the police," Lottie said, pulling her cell phone out of her pocket. "Gas can? Car in a ditch? It might be nothing, but given that there was a murder on Danielle's farm yesterday, I'd say these are connected."

She walked over to the opposite side of the dirt road, arguing with Shelly, the 911 operator who was, as usual, reluctant to send the limited county police presence to what she always assumed was a waste of time. The woman annoyed me, but I understood that she was trying to keep the sheriff and his two deputies, one of whom was unofficial, from racing around the county on fools' errands. The sheriff didn't seem to respond to even a potential murder call, and Jake was retired and supposed to be only pulled in when needed. That left poor Sean dealing with the majority of the county's policing requirements.

I winced, wondering if Sean was okay after his close-encounter with Squeakers yesterday. Had he truly had broken a rib? If the only official deputy was injured, and the sheriff was off having a steak somewhere, then that would leave Jake to respond.

Sure enough, it wasn't a deputy's vehicle that slowly pulled down the bumpy dirt road in the next twenty minutes, but a truck, lifted and fully capable of dealing with the terrain. Danielle had risked the poison ivy to make her way toward us, and we all clustered together, watching as Jake climbed out of his truck.

"So you got the short stick again?" I called out to him.

"Seems to be happening a whole lot the last few months," he replied. "What did you ladies find?"

We showed Jake the vehicle then I led him over to the gas can. He made notes, then called for a tow and for Stef. We hung around as he took pictures with his cell phone and explored the vehicle with gloved hands, wading through the briars and weeds. He called the tags as well as the VIN number into the office, shining his flashlight through the windows and under the car as he checked everything out.

"Is Deputy Sean okay?" I asked, recognizing the voice on the other end of his phone call.

"Bruised ribs." Jake stood and looked through the window into the back seat of the vehicle. "Way more painful than it sounds, so he's on desk duty. He *should* be off, but Sean feels bad about me having to cover for him, so he's still technically working."

"The sheriff should feel equally bad about you covering for him," I snapped, annoyed at the elected official that I hadn't been a resident to vote for. This coming fall's election, I was *not* going to cast a vote for that guy. I didn't care if I had to write in a random name, I wasn't giving my approval for a man who valued his meals above investigating a murder scene.

"After forty years of working in law enforcement I've learned not to get twisted up over some political yahoo with his or her own agenda," Jake commented as he circled around to the trunk. He glanced down at his phone as it beeped, then nodded. "Looks like the car was registered to Wilber Kendricks. Not a state-owned vehicle, but his personal one."

I frowned. "Is that usual? Do inspectors drive their own cars, or should they be in something more official?"

Jake waved a hand back toward his own truck. "Clearly it's not that unusual. I'm showing up to crime scenes in my personal vehicle. From what I know about the state marijuana program, it's a new department. I doubt there's the budget for state vehicles at this point. They probably had the guy submit for mileage reimbursement, like I do."

"I can't see a reason for Wilber Kendricks to drive a sedan off-road, park in this remote location, and hike through weeds to inspect a field he has every right to survey," I commented. "I'm assuming his killer took Kendricks's car from Danielle's driveway and ditched it here."

"Either that or the killer had an accomplice who helped ditch the car," Jake said.

"I'd assumed the killer had his own vehicle parked near Danielle's drive, but maybe this is how they came onto the property," I suggested. "There's the gas can and trampled path leading from this road to Danielle's pot field. Whoever killed Kendricks might have parked here, hiked across the field, killed the inspector, then driven the victim's car here to ditch before taking his own vehicle home."

Lottie nodded. "If he was in a hurry to get going after killing the inspector, then taking the victim's car to drive back here would be a lot faster than hiking across the field to retrieve his own car."

"Plus, hiding the car might have been a way to delay Danielle's finding the body," Sierra added. "If she got home to find a car in her driveway, she'd wander around the farm looking for whoever was here. Without the car, it might have been hours or even a day or two before she found the body."

"Maybe not a day or two," Danielle chimed in. "I check the field daily for any sign of disease and to check soil moisture. But the body might have been there undiscovered until the morning—especially if it took me a while to fix the tractor and drive it home."

Just then Stef pulled up in a dark blue Suburban with county plates. Two men climbed out of the vehicle and started pulling cases and gear from the back while the town's coroner and paramedic strolled up to us.

"Y'all sure are making me earn my paycheck this week," she commented. "Drake, you take care of pictures then dust for prints. Tad, you're bagging and tagging."

"There's a week's worth of fast-food bags on the floors," Jake told her. "Whoever ditched the car here didn't bother trying to clean it up."

"Then there should be lots of evidence to sort through,"

Stef commented as she snapped on a pair of gloves. "Goodie. Overtime."

Stef didn't sound all that thrilled at the prospect, but given that Jake was working when he was supposed to be retired, she was in good company. I wondered if any of the DNA evidence she found would be from the killer, or if it was all from the inspector. Had the killer wiped down the tamping rod before placing it in Danielle's barn? Or had he worn gloves during the whole thing? I glanced at the car, thinking there might not be much there to identify the murderer, unless the labs were as thorough as they were on the television crime shows.

"I'll go ahead and look at the gas can first," Stef announced. "This car is gonna take a while, then we'll have to get it towed to impound and do another sweep. After Jake has your statements and is done with you, you all can go on home. No sense in everyone hanging around here for hours if they don't have to."

I felt a bit disappointed, even though I knew watching her staff collect evidence would probably be a bit boring, and I had things to do back at the campground. The others were equally busy, and I knew that Lottie would call me as soon as she found something out through her gossip network, so I led Stef over and showed her where I'd found the gas can.

"Sorry. I picked it up, so it's got my prints on the handle," I told her.

She nodded. "Hopefully we'll find more than yours on here as well. Drake! Put some numbers down and get pictures of any tire tracks. Make sure you get a cast of them as well."

After snapping a few pictures of the gas can, she picked it up and placed it in a giant clear plastic bag. Then she took more pictures of the ground without the can on it, and began looking around the surrounding area, separating weeds and briars with what looked like a hiking pole.

"I'll walk you ladies back to the farm," Jake told us. "I'm gonna need to ask some of the cops from Savage and Derwood if they can come back here this afternoon. Clearly we need to expand our original search area."

"As long as you're careful about the plants," Danielle warned them. "No powders or sprays or anything unless you tell me first. These things are worth a lot, and I don't want my contract in any more jeopardy than it already is."

Jake held up his hand and nodded solemnly. "I promise the other guys and I will take care around your plants, Danielle. Although we might be here pretty late again."

She sighed. "Guess that can't be helped. I'll be glad when the killer is found, this is over, and I can go back to being a regular pot farmer again."

Was there such a thing as a "regular pot farmer"? Either way, I agreed with Danielle. I'd be glad when this case was solved and we could all go back to whatever passed for normal life in Reckless.

CHAPTER 9

"*H*ow'd it go?" Mom asked as I walked into the camp store. "Was our Elvis a rockstar?"

I tied the hound's leash to the hook at his spot behind the register as Mom ruffled his long ears. "Eventually he was. At first he was more interested in tracking cats and the chickens than he was in helping the police find a murderer."

I told her what we'd discovered, and what Jake and Stef had said as I took a quick look around the shop and at the register tape. "How have things been here? Relaxed and slow for once?"

"For once." Mom laughed. "It was a nice break given that we'll be crazy-busy tomorrow. Cabins three, five, and ten told me they plan on heading out right around dusk tonight. I almost didn't want to tell you because I know you'll insist on cleaning those cabins in the middle of the darned night, but I guess work tonight makes less stress tomorrow."

She was right. It *was* less stressful in the long run if I pulled a late-night and got those cabins cleaned right away. Someday I'd be able to afford someone to come in and at least help me clean. Someday I might be able to afford to have someone do *all* the housekeeping, descending on us Thursday around noon with a team and having all dozen cabins spotless with clean linen in less than an hour, while I sat on my porch and drank iced tea. But today was not that day.

I scratched my arm, daydreaming of a future where the campground was less work and more fun, and knowing full well that day might be far in the future, or may never come at all.

Scratching. Drat. I looked down at my arm and saw two red dots by my wrist, and another two on the back of my hand. As if on cue, I felt a few places on my ankle begin to itch as well.

"Got into some poison ivy over at that farm?" Mom leaned over to see the splotches and shook her head with a "tsk" noise. "Guess I better get the Aqua Net out from under the bathroom sink. It's the season. Mickey Marx was in earlier to buy Benadryl. Her arms were covered in Calamine lotion, poor thing."

We'd need to order some small bottles of Calamine to keep here in the camp store as well as more antihistamines. And mini bottles of hair spray.

"They must have some alien-level poison ivy here in Reckless," I complained, trying not to scratch. "Normally it takes a few days for me to get a rash, and it's never more than one or two spots. I hope I didn't suddenly get Dad's sensitivity to the plants after all these years."

"It could be a reaction to something else," Mom pointed out. "There's poison sumac and poison oak around here as well as stinging nettle. And lots of people get rashes from those Mayapple plants as well."

Great. Hopefully hairspray would be just as effective on those as it was on a poison ivy spots. I came out from behind the counter and searched the shelves, pulling a box of

Benadryl down and reading the back. The stuff always made me a little sleepy, but I didn't have any of the other brands of antihistamine in the store or back at the house, and I knew that Benadryl worked.

"Can you mark this box down as an owner comp in the inventory?" I asked as I popped one of the pink pills in my mouth. "You said we have some hairspray back at the house? In the bathroom in the cabinet under the sink?"

"I'm sure we do but…." Mom pulled her purse from under the counter and began to dig through it. "Oh good! I found it. Here." Mom pulled a small bottle of hairspray out and handed it to me. "It's probably ten years old, and it's not Aqua Net, but it should hold you off until you get a chance to swing by the house."

I took the bottle and shook it, noting that there was hardly anything left. "Sheesh Mom. You need to clean out your purse more often than once a decade. I can't believe you've been lugging this around for so long. It's almost empty."

"You never know when hairspray will come in handy," she countered. "Taming a wild lock of hair. Treating poison ivy. Fighting off an assailant."

"With half a squirt of hairspray?" I pressed the plunger a dozen times just to get a few sprays onto my wrist. "I hope you have better self-defense items in your purse, or you're going to be in trouble."

I'd taken to carrying pepper spray when I went around the campground at night as well as on hikes after I'd had a run-in with a murderer the first month we'd bought the campground. Maybe Mom should do the same. For a small town, Reckless seemed to have a lot of crime—especially since I'd arrived. I'd like to think it was a coincidence, an unusual spike, and that things would soon return to normal, but I worried. Maybe it was me. Although, to be fair, the first murder had happened before we'd actually signed the documents taking ownership of the campground. Plus, my business and I could hardly be blamed for a state inspector being killed on a farm miles away.

"I did a little digging while you were out," Mom said, interrupting my thoughts. "It was slow, and I was curious, so I started reading about all the laws and regulations governing legal marijuana production in Virginia. Then I decided to see what I could find on Wilber Kendricks. Did you know he's a local? At least he used to be. He grew up in Derwood."

"Seriously?" I sat down, eager to hear more. If Kendricks was a local, maybe his murder had nothing at all to do with Danielle or with her pot plants.

Mom nodded, pulling up something on her tablet and handing it over. The device showed an unflattering black-and-white picture from a high school yearbook. Wilber Kendricks. Class of '83. General curriculum. Yearbook committee in tenth grade. Newsletter committee in tenth and eleventh grade. Ninth grade football.

Pretty average guy. Not academic, not really a jock, and not much of a joiner in terms of clubs. None of that was a big mark against the man, though. I had plenty of friends in high school who cruised through their teens in the academic middle with a decent GPA and few interests. The picture was horrible, but I didn't know if that reflected on Wilber Kendricks or the photographer. He had brown hair that had been feathered back from a center part. His narrow-set eyes looked shifty, and that fuzzy, not-quite-a-mustache on his upper lip gave me the overall impression of "future used-car salesman."

"His family is still in the area," Mom continued. "His mother passed away a while ago, but his father lives at the Derwood Retirement Community. He's got a sister who lives over in Savage—she's married with three grown kids and has a grandson that was born in January. According to public records, Wilber Kendricks had married right out of high school. It looks like his wife and he moved to Roanoke shortly after the wedding where he got a job as a county health inspector. They had a daughter a few years later, then were divorced around their five year anniversary. The wife returned to Derwood after their divorce while he climbed the government-job ladder in health inspections, then in alcohol/tobacco inspections for the state."

I laughed. "Gosh Mom. Stalker much?"

"Absolutely." She grinned. "There's a ton of publicly available information, and if the government and companies can't invest in minimal internet security, then it's on them if I find information they should have put behind a decent firewall."

"Do not go getting arrested, Mom," I warned her, worried that I'd need to post bail for my eighty-five-year-old mother. The thought of her doing a perp-walk, of spending even a night in jail made me shudder.

"Pffft. Like anyone is going to arrest some old woman for 'accidentally' stumbling into their employee database." The little air quotes she made around the word "accidentally" didn't exactly reassure me.

"So the inspector has ties to this area," I mused. "That changes things. I wonder who else has a motive to want him dead? Angry ex-wife? That sister, or maybe her husband? A high-school classmate who's been harboring a grudge for the last forty years?"

"Unless something happened recently to set her off, I doubt it's the ex-wife. I mean, the year when the divorce is going through seems like it would be the prime time for a murder attempt, not decades later."

I grabbed a sheet of paper off of the printer and started to make some notes. "Maybe something *did* happen recently. When did his mother pass away? Maybe there was a dispute over the estate or a disagreement at her funeral that unearthed a long-buried feud in the family."

Mom frowned in thought. "The mother passed seven years ago, and from what I could see, everything went to the father. There aren't any records of legal action between the two siblings, but that doesn't mean they didn't have a spat over the funeral. Although, just like the divorce, it seems odd that the sister would act on a disagreement with her brother seven years after their mother died."

Even so, I jotted down a few notes about the sister and the mother. "You said Wilber and his wife had a child? She would probably be in her thirties by now."

Mom nodded. "A daughter. She's thirty-five, single, and living in Chicago. Degree in art history. Runs a small gallery on the northside."

I stared at my mother, a little unnerved at her investigative skills and impressed by what she'd been able to dig up between selling guests coffee and convenience packs, and boat rentals.

"Wilber's ex returned to Derwood after they divorced, as I mentioned before. Her name is Marsha. She kept her married name of Kendricks, but that's not unusual. I know lots of people who did that for the children."

I hadn't, but then again, my ex had cheated on me and left me for another woman. I didn't want to be carrying his last name any longer than I had to. Colter had his father's name, of course, but none of the teachers, or school administrators had found it all that difficult to keep track of our difference in surnames.

Not everyone made that choice in a divorce, though.

"Marsha Kendricks." I frowned, knowing I'd heard that name before.

"She works at the county co-op," Mom said. "Never remarried. Owns a little ranch house in the Mapleton subdivision in Derwood. Woman really has a lead foot from all the speeding tickets on her record. How she manages to get that ancient Geo Metro of hers over the speed limit is beyond me."

"Mom, you're scaring me," I told her.

She nodded. "Understandable. I scare myself sometimes. But back to Wilber Hendricks, I don't see Marsha as the killer. The divorce was too long ago. Their daughter is grown, on her own, and seven hundred miles away. Marsha has a pretty decent life in Derwood from what I can see. Besides, if she wanted to kill Wilber, I get the feeling she'd run him over with her Geo Metro rather than follow him to an inspection site, and bash him in the head."

"True." I looked down at my notes and the list of potential suspects, then put an "x" next to Marsha's name. I still wasn't ruling her or any of Kendricks's family out, but without any evidence that there was a family feud going on, they weren't particularly strong suspects. It was more likely that Wilber's murder *was* related to his work as a cannabis investigator for the state.

Up until this morning, the top suspect was probably Danielle. There was a lot in that theory that didn't fit, but the murder did occur on her property and Wilber Kendricks would have held the success of her business in the palm of his hand. A problematic inspection, a report of irregularities, would have jeopardized Danielle's contract. It was a reasonable motive for murder, even if the timing was an issue.

But now... The gas can. The multiple tire tracks. The ditched vehicle. The path Elvis had taken across the field indicated that Hendricks had done the same, and it had put us on track to where we'd found the evidence today. It all pointed to the inspector being murdered by someone who was there to vandalize Danielle's crop.

There were a few holes in that theory as well, though. Did

Kendricks chase the man off, then the saboteur doubled back around to kill the inspector and hide his car? It still seemed an extreme action to take when the guy could have just driven off. Kendricks probably would have discussed the need for additional security with Danielle, but I doubted he would have seen enough to actually get the trespasser charged. Why add murder onto your list of crimes when trespass and maybe intent-to-vandalize would have been the maximum the intruder would have faced—if he'd even faced that at all.

Still, it was somewhere to start. And at the very least, today's discoveries shifted suspicion away from Danielle and onto someone else.

CHAPTER 10

$\mathcal{M}$om and I had just finished up a quick dinner, and I was gathering my supplies and products for some late-night cabin cleaning, when Lottie pulled up to the house. Elvis jumped from his cushion, running to the door and bouncing up and down with excitement. Whoever had labeled hounds as lazy had only gotten half the picture. When they were at rest, they were totally at rest. They snored, sprawled out on the sofa, or their beds, or on a sunny patch of grass with their ears flopped over their eyes and long legs everywhere. Elvis took any opportunity to snooze, but all I needed to do was mention a walk, or dinner, or that magic word "ball" and he was awake and on his feet in a split-second. Same if someone he knew and liked came to the door. My bloodhound was happy to greet all the new campers each week, and might open an eye if someone paused to scratch behind his ears or rub his belly as he slept, but there were certain people he considered worth fully waking up for. Jake was one of those people, and so was Lottie.

I opened the door and ushered my neighbor in as Elvis

circled around her legs, beating her with his tail. "Here to help me clean cabins?" I teased.

"Nope. I'm here to take you to a CAD meeting." Lottie smiled at my mother. "Unless Ellie Mae is heading out to play bridge or go to her knitting club."

Mom waved a hand. "My knitting group meets Sunday afternoons, and I'm an alternate for a bridge team this Monday night, so I'm in for the evening. I'm happy to stay here if you and Sassy want to go out."

"I was out all day Tuesday, and again this afternoon," I protested. "I feel bad leaving you with the campground tonight."

Mom lifted an eyebrow. "You worked Tuesday morning until nine, and you were back to work in the evening, so technically you did *not* take Tuesday off. And you were only gone for a few hours this afternoon, which is our slowest day of the week. You're owed a few extra hours here and there, Sassy. And I think it's good for you to be expanding your hobbies. Go to this computer aided design meeting with Lottie. Maybe you can work on plans for a new boathouse or something."

I frowned at her, confused for a moment. Then I realized she was referring to the anachronym. "This CAD isn't an architectural software, it stands for Citizens Against Drugs."

Mom's eyes widened. "Are drugs a problem in Reckless? I know that even small rural communities aren't shielded from the drug epidemic, but I hadn't realized it was serious enough to warrant a non-profit action committee."

"The group is more about prevention and education," Lottie explained. "The founder lost a close friend to a drug overdose, so it's personal to her. I'm not a huge fan of Gwen Sarlet, but I get why she founded CAD. And while I think some of their views and actions are a little over-the-top, there *is* a need for awareness, even in a small community like

Reckless. We have our fair share of addicts here, and while the town might not be a hotbed of drug distribution activity, it's still a problem."

"Do you think this group had something to do with Wilber Kendricks's murder?" Mom regarded us with a narrow-eyed expression. "Because I seriously doubt you two have suddenly decided to help make anti-drug pamphlets for high school kids."

"Maybe they did have something to do with the murder. I figured it wouldn't hurt to nose around," Lottie told her. "The police are running finger prints and checking out the tire tracks, but there's nothing saying we can't show up at a CAD meeting and see who looks suspicious. Besides, Marla Johnson always brings cookies. That alone is worth listing to Gwen Sarlet for an hour."

I eyed my cleaning supplies as Lottie spoke, torn between duty and curiosity. I should stay here and spend a few hours ironing out details for the Friday night campground activities, and cleaning the cabins once the early checkout folks left.

But in all honesty, there wasn't that much left to organize for Friday's sunset paint-and-sip, or the kids' balloon sculpture activity. The earliest of the early checkouts wasn't for another hour at least, so I couldn't start cleaning cabins right now anyway. I could go to the CAD meeting with Lottie, and still be home in time to clean.

Minutes later we were on our way.

As we pulled into the parking lot of the community center, I noted quite a few cars in the spaces. Instead of heading immediately inside, Lottie took a little notepad and pen from her giant purse and began walking around between the cars.

"What are you doing?" I asked as I followed her.

"Whoever parked down that dirt road to access

Danielle's field needed a four-wheel drive with some decent clearance. And they probably have mud on their tires and wheel wells, although I'm writing down the tag and description for the clean trucks as well. The murderer might have run it though a car wash in the last twenty-four hours, so I'm not going to rule out anyone who has a clean truck."

Lottie was much better at this whole amateur detective thing than I was. Following her lead, I pulled a notepad and pen out of my own purse and took the other end of the parking lot. By the time we met in the middle we both had descriptions and tags for a total of six vehicles.

"Do you recognize any of them?" I asked Lottie, figuring as a long-term resident of the area she might know people's vehicles as well as anybody.

She nodded. "Two of the trucks I don't know but these four I do." She reached over to cross two of the vehicles off my list. "Tracy Bowen was working Tuesday at the Chat-n-Chew. I saw her there that morning, and I know she was doing the six-to-two shift. And Roddy Trueman is ninety-five if he's a day, with a portable oxygen tank. No way that man was tromping through briars carrying a full gas can in one hand and his oxygen tank in another.

"So we're down to four," I commented. "Tell me about the two you recognize."

"The white SUV is Gwen's," Lottie said with a knowing nod. "The blue truck belongs to Scat Johnson."

"Scat?" It didn't seem like the sort of name a person who was a member of an anti-drug group would have.

"I think his real name is Schroeder, but he's been Scat since kindergarten. He works at the hospital in Derwood, but does ten-hour shifts Thursday through Sunday, so he would have been off Tuesday. That big truck of his could absolutely navigate the dirt road, and it's covered in dried mud. Of course, Scat likes to go off-roading when he's not working, so a muddy truck isn't exactly incriminating."

"So... Gwen, Scat, or two people we don't know," I mused.

Lottie held up a finger. "I probably know them, I just don't recognize their vehicles. Let's go inside. We'll catch the last twenty minutes of the meeting, then eat cookies and see if anyone looks guilty. Plus, we can watch as people leave and discover who those other two trucks belong to."

It was a good plan, and I was really wanting to try Marla Johnson's famous cookies.

Lottie and I circled around to the front of the community center, went inside, then headed down the hall to the meeting room. A woman who looked to be in her late forties stood up on the stage. Gwen Sarlet had shoulder-length, auburn hair, and was dressed casually in jeans and a T-shirt. I listened to her speak about prescription Adderall abuse in teens as we took our seats and looked around.

A dozen people sat on folding metal chairs, half of them paying attention to Gwen and the other half eyeing their phones. Off to the side of the room was a long table with a plastic tablecloth covered in bright yellow sunflowers. It held two large urns for coffee, a few bowls of chips and pretzels, and a giant platter with an assortment of cookies stacked high. I swear I could smell the sugar and melted chocolate from where I sat.

None of the attendees looked like a killer to me, but clearly I wasn't attuned to these sorts of things. A few did look like they were stressed or nervous, but that might have had nothing at all to do with the murder at Danielle's farm.

Twenty minutes later Gwen ended the meeting after having assigned pamphlet distribution to four people as well as putting Marla Johnson in charge of creating signs for a planned trip to Roanoke to picket a dispensary. The crowd rushed to the cookies, and I held back, resisting the urge to dive into the mob and grab a few of my own. There had to be five dozen cookies on that platter. Surely there would be one or two left over for me after the actual CAD members got done.

"Did you see Scat?" Lottie whispered. "He kept looking at the door like he expected the police to come through any moment. The guy nearly jumped out of his skin when we walked in."

"He's the blond hipster guy in the red flannel shirt?" I whispered back.

Lottie nodded, and I took a better look at Scat Johnson. He did seem nervous. The guy wasn't even getting a cookie, and if that didn't indicate guilt, then I didn't know what did. To prove my own innocence, I made my way over to the crowd and grabbed one of the snickerdoodles from the rapidly diminishing pile of treats. Lottie took a chocolate chip. Then as she went to speak with Gwen, I headed for Scat.

"Hi." I held out my hand, noting that the guy spun around in a panic at my greeting. "I'm Sassy Letouroux."

"Scat Johnson." He shook my hand, shooting a quick glance at the doorway. "Letouroux? Aren't you the woman who bought Len Trout's campground?"

"I am." I scrambled to think of a reason for me to be here. "I don't have any loved ones who have been impacted by drugs, but I know that they can devastate even a small community."

He nodded and it was clear I'd gotten his attention even though he still kept glancing toward the door. "It's not just a big-city problem anymore. Rural communities have citizens that struggle with addiction too. And addiction doesn't only affect young people or the homeless either. So many families have a brother or cousin or even a parent hooked on prescription drugs."

"Did you struggle with addiction? Or someone in your family?" I asked, feeling that there was some personal background to Scat's passionate speech.

He swallowed a few times, looking once more at the doorway. "My cousin. And me. When he died of an overdose…well, that was what made me decide to get clean. It's been three years this past March."

"I'm sorry for your loss. And you should be very proud of yourself," I told him. "Three years clean is no small feat."

There were tears in his eyes when his met my gaze. "I dedicate every day to Simon. And I'll do everything I can to make sure no family loses someone they love to drugs or alcohol."

"Is that why you went out to Danielle's farm Tuesday, to burn her marijuana crop?"

His eyes widened at my words.

"I understand your motive, but Danielle is no more to blame than Bobbi Benjamin over at the Bait and Beer, or whoever owns the Twelve Gauge are for alcohol-related deaths. Pot is legal, and unless citizens convince the state of Virginia to reverse that decision, Danielle is just a woman growing a legal crop under contract from the state."

His face reddened. "I didn't…It wasn't… It's a drug, just like all the others. And alcohol is just as bad. If Danielle was a good person, she'd stick to soybeans and corn."

"A fire could have killed her livestock, burned her other fields, burned down her house and barns, and maybe even spread to neighboring farms," I pointed out, noticing that our conversation was drawing some attention.

"She had cameras up, you know," Lottie chimed in. "After the other vandalism attempts, she put cameras long the fence line."

"I twisted them around," Scat said. "And it wouldn't have been a big fire. The plants are green and it's rained recently, so only the ones I doused would have burned. It wouldn't have spread. Plus, Danielle would have noticed it before hardly more than a quarter of an acre had burned. Her livestock, buildings and other crop wouldn't have been in danger."

"But Danielle wasn't there to notice," Lottie pointed out. "She was in town helping get Squeakers off a porch roof. And her field is mulched with straw. It would have burned and spread farther than you're thinking."

"Scat, how could you," Gwen scolded. "We're a peaceful group. We protest. We educate. We write our elected officials. We don't destroy people's property or threaten their livelihoods. I was working to convince Danielle to give up farming pot through persuasion. There was no need to try to set fire to her field."

Scat's jaw twitched. "Simon died. He died. And I was on that path to death myself. Pamphlets and picketing and writing letters isn't enough. We have to *do* something. We have to stop it before more people die."

"One more person did die, and it was because of you," I said, pushing Scat to admit to murder as well as the attempted vandalism. "We know the reason you didn't end up setting fire to the field. It was because the cannabis inspector saw you with your gas can. He chased you away, but he saw you and knew what you were going to do. So you circled back around to the farm, grabbed Danielle's tamping rod out of the barn, then hit him with it. You murdered him so he couldn't identify you."

It didn't sound right. It hadn't sounded right when I'd worked through that theory earlier today, and it *still* didn't sound right. Why murder someone to cover up what would have been a misdemeanor trespass at worst? Why not just get in the truck and drive away?

Scat sucked in a panicked breath, looking around at the

meeting attendees all focused on him before glancing once more at the door. "I didn't kill anyone. I did go to Danielle's a few times and damage her plants, just to warn her off growing that stuff. I did go there Tuesday to burn some of her crop. And I ran when that man saw me and came after me. But I didn't kill him. I just ditched the gas can in the weeds, got in my truck and went home. I didn't kill that man."

"It looks bad, Scat," Lottie pointed out. "You were there. The inspector chased you off. They found his car down a ditch right near where you left the gas can—which probably has your fingerprints all over it. There were tire tracks that I'm sure will match those on your truck."

"Was it self-defense?" Gwen asked. "Did the inspector catch up with you and attack you? Did he threaten you?"

Scat shook his head. "No! I swear I didn't kill him. I didn't even touch him. He yelled at me, and I ran. I ran, ditched the gas can, got in my truck and left. And I haven't been back since then. I did not kill that man."

Out of the corner of my eye I saw two men come into the meeting room. In the lead was Sheriff Oliver, and behind him was Deputy Sean. I waited, surprised not to see Jake with them. Hopefully the poor guy had the evening off after spending the day collecting evidence.

"Scat," the sheriff called out, one hand on the stick looped in his duty belt. "Schroeder Johnson, you're under arrest for criminal trespass."

"And murder," one of the CAD attendees called out. "You need to arrest him for murder as well."

Lottie and I stepped back. I didn't think they could arrest Scat for murder yet, although he probably *was* a suspect. Unless the techs and Jake had found additional evidence, there couldn't possibly be enough to charge him with *that* crime.

And call me crazy, but I didn't think Scat did it. The logistics didn't line up, and strangely I believed the guy. He was nervous, anxious about getting caught for what he'd done, but he confessed pretty quickly at my inexpert questioning. I believed him when he said he hadn't murdered the inspector. From my brief knowledge of him, Scat seemed like the runaway type, not the sneak-back-and-murder-someone type.

Lottie and I held back, watching as Sean cuffed Scat and read him his rights.

They'd caught the man who'd been vandalizing Danielle's marijuana crop, but I truly believed they hadn't caught Wilber Kendricks's murderer.

CHAPTER 11

"I never would have thought that Scat could possibly kill someone. But then again, I never imagined he'd try to burn Danielle's crop either." Gwen hugged herself, rubbing her arms.

Lottie and I had stayed, even after Scat had been taken away in cuffs and Marla Johnson had left with her empty platter. The other CAD members had been just as shocked as Gwen.

"Maybe it wasn't Scat," I said.

"He fessed up pretty quick to the vandalism," Lottie pointed out. "So maybe he was telling the truth about not being the killer."

I remembered what Jake had said at the crime scene, and what Lottie had relayed from her contact at the coroner's office. There had been defensive wounds on Wilber Kendricks's arms and body. The killer hadn't just hit him in self-defense or in an attempt to get away. They'd hit him multiple times. Then stuck around to both plant the tamping rod and move Kendricks's car. That suggested either premeditation or a level of thinking after the fact that was clearly calculated.

And the tamping rod... Danielle admitted it was hers. The police had found it in the barn. It would have been in plain sight there, but not at all handy if a person needed to suddenly defend themselves out at the edge of a crop field. That meant the killer had purposely gone into the barn to get a weapon before he'd had the altercation with Wilber Kendricks. It definitely showed premeditation to some degree.

It was possible that Scat was chased away by Kendricks, then drove around to the front of the farm, got the tamping rod out of the barn, killed the inspector, and planted the rod before ditching Kendricks's car, jogging across the field and driving his own vehicle away, but that would have taken time —time that Scat would have been in danger of getting caught by a returning Danielle. But as I'd thought so many times before, why kill the inspector over what at most would have been simple trespass? Especially when there was a good chance Kendricks wouldn't have bothered to file a police report, or have seen enough of Scat to identify him. It didn't fit.

"If it wasn't Scat, then we need to go back to other motives and other potential killers. Like that the killer was someone who didn't get the contract to grow pot," Lottie suggested. "An angry competitor that's trying to frame Danielle for the murder, or at least get her contract canceled. It could have been the same scenario we're suggesting with Scat, only someone with more to lose—someone Kendricks knew, could identify, and who'd be facing the loss of their entire business instead of just facing a trespass charge."

"A big, multi-state grower? Those are all large corporations." Gwen looked doubtful. "I can't see a corporation risking a murder charge over one contract in Virginia—especially if they've got contracts in states all up and down the east coast. It's just one contract."

I held up my hands, because we had no evidence to support any of these ideas. "How about an illegal grower, then? Someone who resented not just the competition that Danielle's crop posed, but the competition of the state of Virginia?"

Gwen slowly shook her head. "If we were talking heroin or cocaine, maybe. Pot is big money, but the trend toward decriminalization has been going on for over a decade. Hitting a small local grower by killing the inspector seems like it would be a futile action. Besides, an illegal grower would have more opportunity, not less with the state dispensaries in play. Legalization of pot actually expands usage to people who would normally never buy a bag from a dealer. The dispensaries limit purchase volume each month, so there will be increased demand but also a cap on a user's ability to buy legally. Yes, there's competition from the state, but there's also an increase in potential customers for non-legal dealers."

She was right. And just like with Scat, I couldn't see a local small-time grower risking everything to murder an inspector who was out surveying a crop under contract with the state. Unless Wilber Kendricks knew about the illegal grower and was maybe blackmailing him? That might have given someone enough incentive to commit murder.

That idea had me wondering what sort of person Wilber Kendricks was. I remembered the shifty eyes from his high school graduation photo, and considered once more that there could be all sorts of things in the man's personal life that might make him a target for murder.

With no answers, Lottie and I headed home. The closer we got to the campground, the more I dreaded the long night of cleaning ahead of me. By the time we'd parked in front of the house, I was downright grumpy at the thought of scrubbing floors and washing sheets.

"Thanks for driving tonight," I told Lottie as I unbuckled my seatbelt. To my surprise, she shut off her car, and unbuckled herself as well.

"Did…did you want to come inside to talk, or for a cup of coffee?" I asked her trying to hide my dismay. Lottie was a friend, and normally I'd be more hospitable, but I had cabins to clean, and if I didn't get to them soon, there was a good chance I'd fall asleep while doing it.

"I won't say no to coffee, but we should probably put them in go-cups and get started. I turn into a pumpkin after two in the morning." She laughed at my confused expression. "You didn't think I'd drop you off and go home while you stay up late to clean cabins, did you? I dragged you away from your work to play amateur sleuth. The least I can do is help you change sheets, dust, and mop."

I blew out a relieved breath. "Lottie you're a saint. Thank you. I really could use the help tonight, but won't Scotty be expecting you home?"

"Oh. He's away on a business trip this week." She waved a hand. "No one is home waiting up for me. That means I absolutely can help my friend."

I wasn't sure what Lottie's husband did for a living, but it seemed to involve a lot of travel. I'd never actually met him, although I had seen him leaving the house once when I was pulling down Lottie's driveway to drop off her casserole dish. Scotty was a tall, good-looking man with an athletic build, and a head full of dark hair. He'd been carrying a briefcase and had waved when I'd beeped hello, but he hadn't waited to actually meet me or talk. Lottie was in her early fifties, so I'd assumed Scotty must be about the same age. He certainly hadn't looked much older than her from the quick glimpse I'd gotten of him that one day.

It was a shame he was gone so much for work, but some jobs required a lot of travel, and he was probably giving it his all in a push for them to be financially secure for retirement. Not everyone was like me and planning to work until their last breath. Hopefully he'd have some vacation time, or at least a few days at home where I could invite him and Lottie over for dinner one night and properly meet my friend's husband.

"Thank you," I told Lottie again. "Let's grab some coffee and the supplies and get started. With two of us cleaning, we should be done by midnight at the latest."

Mom was still awake. She put a pot of coffee on and chatted with Lottie while I took Elvis for a quick walk to relieve himself and sniff all the millions of smells that intrigued a bloodhound. The coffee was finished by the time we returned. Mom had already fixed go-cups for both Lottie and me, so we wished her and Elvis a good night, grabbed our caffeine and the cleaning supplies, and headed out.

Lottie got right to work with the lemony polish on the wood furniture while I quickly stripped the bed and put the dirty linens on the front porch to take over to the laundry.

Lottie swept and mopped while I ran the linens over and put them in the washer, returning with a clean set from the supply closet. After making the bed, we gathered up the supplies and locked the door, then made our way to the next cabin. We'd cleaned that first cabin in record time. Having Lottie help me made me realize that it would be good to hire someone to assist with the cleaning duties, even if I couldn't afford to completely outsource this activity yet. Someday I'd be able to pay a cleaning crew to descend on the cabins and be in and out in an hour with everything sparkling and fresh, but for now, I needed to save money and do it myself. But school was almost out for the summer, and I might be able to afford a teen who was looking to make some extra money as a helper. I had Austin working here. Sierra's daughter worked for her coffee shop and delivered food to the campground. I was sure one of them would know of another motivated, hardworking teen who'd be willing to do some cleaning once or twice a week.

"How's the dress hunting going?" I asked, thinking it would be nice to pass the time with some conversation. "Has Amanda made a decision yet?"

"Here's the latest." Lottie pulled out her phone. I set down the pile of sheets and went over to look at the image.

"I like it." The dress was high-necked in sheer fabric with floral lace in an A-line, ending in an explosion of fabric at the ankle that made Amanda look like a virginal mermaid.

"She can't decide between this one and the gauzy Grecian-style one." Lottie sighed. "She wants to buy both, then decide closer to the wedding."

I choked a little at that. "She wants to buy *both*?" I squeaked.

Wedding dresses were insanely expensive. Two wedding dresses was over-the-top. Plus, what would Amanda do with the spare? It wasn't like life offered much occasion to wear a wedding dress outside of your actual wedding. Did she plan on selling it as a consignment for half the original price?

What a horrible waste of her parents' money. I hated to judge a woman I'd never met, but Lottie's daughter was beginning to sound like a Bridezilla.

"That's not all." Lottie put the phone away and faced me. "Suddenly she's thinking about having a destination wedding in Aruba or St. John, and the cost is…well, expensive. Plus, I already put a deposit down on the venue she said she wanted, and I don't think I can get that deposit back."

"Did you give her a budget?" I asked, since that's what I'd done for Colter and Greg's wedding. "You and Scotty decide what your limit is. Tell her she has that amount and share a running tab with her that includes deductions for what you've already spent in deposits, etc. That way if she wants to buy two wedding dresses, she'll either have to cut back on flowers or catering or the band. Or chip in her own money."

"We did have a budget, but.... I hate Instagram and Pinterest," Lottie blew out an exasperated breath. "All these social media influencers and reality shows with their over-the-top weddings. Normal people can't afford that. Normal people shouldn't have to feel like they need to spend that."

"Normal people shouldn't expect a Kardashian wedding," I agreed. "And you're right, things used to be a lot simpler when we didn't have a parade of excess on television and on social media every second of every day. I had a cousin who got married thirty years ago at the local park in the big gazebo they use for summer bands. The reception was a picnic at the same park with a rented pavilion. She and her fiancé did the catering themselves and the whole wedding party helped out the night before, rolling luncheon meat for the sandwich platters and making potato salad."

Lottie laughed. "That sounds really nice, but Amanda would never speak to me again if I made her roll her own luncheon meat the night before the wedding."

I smiled in sympathy. "I'm not saying that's what Amanda should do. I'm just telling you about a nice wedding I went to where there was a *very* limited budget. Everyone had a wonderful time. And I'm sure everyone will have a wonderful time at Amanda's wedding with whatever budget you and Scotty have set."

Lottie sighed. "She was always Scotty's baby girl. He could never deny her anything. We really spoiled her when she was young, so it's not like I shouldn't have seen this sort of thing coming. It's just every time I try to talk to Scotty about the budget, he's too busy or he just tells me to handle it. I'm afraid if I put my foot down on the limit and about some things, that Amanda will just go to her father. Then I'll look like the horrible parent who is a cheapskate when it comes to her daughter's wedding."

I started to say something, then just shut my mouth. Lottie didn't talk a lot about her husband—which was different than every other married woman I knew. Scotty never seemed to be home, never was available to join us for dinner or drinks or anything. Theirs didn't seem like a healthy marriage in my opinion, but who was I to judge? My marriage had imploded decades ago, and I didn't have any other personal experience to compare this marriage to. Still, it was sad to think that Scotty would tell Lottie to handle everything as far as their daughter's wedding and refuse to be involved, only to not support Lottie if Amanda complained.

Plus, it sounded as if this sort of thing had happened in the past. And that put another strike against Scotty in my book. Yep. He was beginning to sound like a total jerk.

"Maybe if I point out that a lot of her friends and extended family won't be able to make the wedding if she has it on some Caribbean island, it will change her mind," Lottie said. "Amanda always wanted a big wedding. She'd be bummed if half the guest list couldn't make it."

"That might work," I told her, thinking that getting a passport, paying for the flight and a more expensive hotel plus a longer stay *would* reduce the number of people responding "yes" for the event.

"And the dresses…" Lottie's voice trailed off.

"*One* dress," I insisted. "Stay strong, Lottie. No bride needs two dresses because she can't make up her mind. Let her attendants vote. Or random TikTok followers. Or she can flip a coin. Don't let her con you into buying two dresses."

I hated confrontation, but even I would hold firm to that one.

Lottie laughed. "You know, the TikTok suggestion might work. At the very least, all the comments and votes might help her make up her mind."

With that she put her phone away and we went back to work, chatting about less controversial topics like the weather, the upcoming town events, and our favorite pizza toppings.

We fell into a routine. Lottie swept and mopped while I grabbed the sheets to take to the wash. Walking in the laundry room door with another load, I heard the whir of the machine going through the spin cycle for the first sheets. Hopefully it would be done by the time I'd thrown these in the second washer, and I could have the first set in the dryer before I left.

My heart sank as I stepped up to the second washer and my foot squished in a puddle of water—sudsy water.

"Drat," I whispered, looking around to see if any campers were approaching for some late-night laundry duty of their own.

No one was in sight, so I threw the dirty sheets in the second washer, then hit pause on the one that was in the middle of a spin cycle before trying to see if I could determine where the water was coming from. It definitely wasn't spilling out of the lid, and although the water on the floor was sudsy, it wasn't bubble-bath-gone-crazy sudsy.

Dragging a stepladder over, I climbed up and leaned over the machine to peer behind the washer. There was a hose coming from the back of the machine that rose from near the bottom then curved to fit down inside a fat PVC pipe. Assuming that was where the water drained, I pulled the hose out and tried to look inside for a clog.

I couldn't see anything blocking either the hose or the

PVC pipe. The pipe didn't have water backed up in it, and nothing dripped out of the hose when I pulled it out, so I was guessing those weren't the problem. Just to be sure, I grabbed an old wire coat hanger that was on the floor of the storage closet, flattened it out, and used it to poke as far as I could into the hose and the PVC pipe.

Nothing. I sighed, looking at the mess on the floor and thinking it must be coming from under the washing machine. That meant it was beyond my limited ability to fix.

With a few grumbled comments about appliances and expenses, I put the clean sheets in a dryer, started the second washer with the dirty sheets, then put an "out of order" sign and a bunch of tape across the top of the broken washer.

Just in case someone else decided to tear the tape and my note off and use the washer anyway, I put the hose back inside the PVC pipe, hoping that would limit the amount of water that would end up on the floor of the laundry room.

I was down to one washer. This wasn't good going into my busy season when there were often anywhere from sixty to eighty people in the campground each week. I'd actually been hoping to add a third washer and dryer to make sure we had plenty of amenities for the campers, but once I'd looked at the cost of the extra plumbing and electric in addition to the machines themselves, I'd decided that project might need to wait until the end of the year. Or later, depending on how the campground finances looked.

And now they were looking worse than they had an hour ago. I'd need to call for a repair person, and hope that I didn't have to replace the washer. So much for getting that hole in my living room ceiling fixed. That too would need to wait. It seemed like every time I started to get a little ahead, something like this happened.

There was no sense dwelling on misfortune when I had stuff to do. Pulling the mop and bucket out of the supply closet, I began to clean the water from the floor. I'd just emptied the bucket and was returning it to the closet when Lottie came through the door of the laundromat, a bundle of dirty sheets in her arms.

"Are you okay?" She blew out a breath and put the sheets on the folding table. "When you didn't come back I got worried. 'Did a bear get her?' I wondered. 'A rabid raccoon? Did she fall into the washing machine and drown?' These were the things going through my head."

I laughed at her list. "The last one is closer to the truth. One of the washers is leaking. I needed to see if it was something I could fix, then clean up the mess. I'm so sorry I made you worry."

And I was also sorry that I'd saddled Lottie with the cabins cleaning solo while I dealt with my washer disaster.

"Just glad you're okay." Lottie walked over to the linen closet and pulled two sets of sheets from it. "I'll go ahead and finish up the cabin I cleaned, then get started on the last one while you do what you need to do here."

"I've done all I can here. I can finish up that last cabin if you need to get home," I told her.

Lottie scowled. "You're not getting rid of me until we're all done. You can get started on that last cabin while I put these sheets on the bed. If we work together we can finish up in another twenty minutes tops, then I can go home and we *both* can go to bed."

I eyed the dirty sheets she'd just brought in and realized that laundry was going to take longer than expected with only one working washer. Even after the cabins were clean and Lottie was gone, I'd need to stay awake and hang around the laundromat. I didn't want to leave sheets in the machines all night. I wanted to make sure the washer and dryers were available for campers tomorrow morning.

But I wasn't going to tell Lottie that. She'd insist on staying, and there was no sense in both of us depriving ourselves of sleep while we waited for my one working washer to finish its cycle.

We got back to work, and sure enough, in less than twenty minutes Lottie was heading down the drive while I waved from the porch of my house.

Then once her taillights vanished from sight, I headed back to the laundromat. There were sheets to wash, and I had at least another hour before the final set was dry, folded, and put into the linen closet.

CHAPTER 12

T wasn't the only one up early the next morning. As Elvis and I did our pre-dawn lap of the campground, we saw people cooking breakfast and organizing belongings for their departure. It was a little bittersweet. Their vacation was over, but by tonight an entire new group would be settling in, ready to enjoy nature and all that my campground had to offer.

I flipped the camp store sign to "Open" at five, but there were only a few early birds getting coffee at that time. It gave me some much-needed peace to go over the schedule for Friday night's activities.

This was the fun part of owning the campground. I had all sorts of things planned for each week. September's Disco Mountain Bike Race already had a dozen entries. I had contracted a local historian for potential "History of Savage Lake" tours if I could manage to get the pontoon boat working. I'd thought that it might also be fun to do a lake ghost tour in the fall. There was the fishing contest, the talent show, inner tube water-gun fights, a wild garlic cooking contest, a chili cookoff, and a "Savage Lake Fishing" lecture complete with a discussion on lures and top fishing spots by Bobbi Benjamin, owner of the Bait and Beer.

This Friday we were going to fire up the bonfire at seven, and start off with a balloon sculpture class for the kids, although I figured some of the adults might join in as well. At eight, there would be a sunset paint-and-sip. The woman I'd hired to lead the guests in their artwork had one picture for the adults to create, and another for any children who might also want to join in. The event was BYOB, but the flyers I'd made up let guests know that we had local wine for sale in the camp store, along with assorted beers and a wide selection of non-alcoholic beverages. Each bottle of wine came with a coupon for a free tasting at the local winery, and I'd get a commission for any purchases made by a guest using their coupon.

It probably wouldn't be enough to repair the washing machine, but every little bit counted.

Grim thoughts of the washing machine sent me to the internet where I began to make a list of local repair companies. I doubted any of them were open this early, but when either Mom or I got a few seconds to breathe later in the morning, one of us would need to start making calls.

On a roll, I went from Googling appliance repair companies to various YouTube videos and articles on what might actually be wrong with the washing machine. I honestly didn't have the time or the skill to fix it myself, but if no one could schedule me for a repair within the next few days, I was absolutely going to try.

Loose or punctured drain hose.

Hmm. I'd checked the hose where it connected to the PVC drainpipe, but obviously hadn't been able to see the portion of hose that went inside the machine. I watched the video of the woman taking the panel off the appliance, locating the broken section, and replacing the hose. It didn't look all that difficult. Once we got all the new guests checked in, maybe I should look and see what it involved. Austin could probably spare a few minutes to help me pull the machine from the wall and get the back panel off once he got here from school. The hose should be cheap, and I was assuming it would be readily available at the home improvement store in Derwood.

Fixing this myself would save me a few hundred dollars—money that could go to repairing that darned hole in my living room ceiling.

Door seal issues. Nope, that couldn't be it. This was a top load washer, and I hadn't seen any sign of leaking from above.

Defective tub seal. I watched that video and grimaced, thinking that might be a little beyond my abilities. Removing the spin basket and turning the washer over? Yikes.

Faulty pressure switch. I wasn't sure what the heck that was, even *after* watching the video. If that was the problem, then I'd need to turn to a professional.

Clogged filter or basket or valve screen. Well, heck. That might be the problem right there. This was a campground and even though we cleaned the washing machines several times a week, there might be dirt, pet hair, or other stuff gunking up the works. That was definitely worth looking into before I shelled out good money to a repair person.

Faulty water pump. That was another one that would have to wait for an actual, qualified repair person to fix.

I eyed the list of appliance repair companies, and decided to see if there was a clog or if the drain hose was to blame before I called one of them in. Thursday was our busiest day, but I needed to somehow squeeze in a few minutes later this morning to attempt to fix the thing myself. If I could, then I'd save some money. If I couldn't, then Mom or I would get to calling and hope that someone could fit us in sometime in the next few days. I didn't like us being down to one washer. If that last one decided to go the way of its buddy and break down as well, then I'd really be in trouble.

Hearing the coffee shop van pulling into the parking area, I minimized my browser tabs, and prepared to begin the morning routine.

I'd barely gotten the food delivery situated before the rush began. Checkout was at noon, but plenty of guests came in early to settle up so they could spend a leisurely morning before heading out. There had been dew on the ground this morning, and quite a few of our tent campers requested wiggle room in their check-out time to ensure their tents were fully dry before they had to break them down and pack them up. Thankfully I could be a bit more flexible about the tent spots, and let the guests know as long as they were out by two, they'd be fine. No one wanted to pack up a wet tent only to have to set it back up to dry once they got home or risk mold.

Some of the RV and camper trailer guests also asked for an extra hour. Turnover would be tight given the number of new guests we had arriving this afternoon, but I said yes to every request. The RV spots required minimal work to prepare, and I was confident that Austin could get everything accomplished in the two hours he had between school ending and check-in. Grass trimming, grill cleaning, trash dumping, and checking the hookups was all he'd really need to do to have those sites ready to go.

It was the cabins that always gave me the most anxiety. Out of the dozen cabins, four were already clean and prepped for new guests thanks to Lottie's and my work last night. Six more guests were checking out today, and I'd need to rush to have those cabins ready for a four o'clock check-in. Thankfully two sets of our guests were staying an extra week, and my cleaning duties today would only be six cabins instead of eight. And thank the Lord for those four guests who'd left last night. I realized there might be a time when I'd need to somehow manage to get twelve cabins cleaned and prepped in less than four hours. When that happened, hopefully I could convince Lottie or Austin or maybe even Flora to give me a hand for some extra money, or in Lottie's case, bribe her with a bottle of wine or dinner.

I needed to look into another teen for help this summer. Plus, once school was out for the year, I'd ask Austin to work a full day on Thursday in addition to some longer hours other days of the week. We'd be busy, and there was only so much Mom and I could do on our own.

I was ringing up coffee and snack purchases for one of the tent campers when the door jingled. I looked up to see Drew and Bree walking into the store followed by Caleb and Courtney. They were all dressed in jeans and long-sleeved shirts with hiking boots and ball caps. I thought it was a bit warm for that sort of hiking attire, then I realized that today was the day for their horseback riding trip.

"Is Landon picking you up here, or are you driving to the ranch?" I asked Caleb as he looked through the day-old pastry basket next to the register.

"We're driving out," Caleb said. "Thought it would be a good idea for us grab a few snacks, just in case we decide to hike after the ride. And Courtney needs some Benadryl. She's got the mother of all poison ivy cases."

Poor thing. My own poison ivy itched at the reminder. It did seem to be the season for it, I thought, remembering that Mom had said that one of our other guests, Mickey, had a bad case of it as well.

"I don't want Benadryl. It'll put me to sleep and I'll fall off my horse." Courtney bent down to lift the cuff of her jeans and scratch at a sock-covered ankle. "Do you have some other type of antihistamine?"

"All we've got is Benadryl." I reached in my bag and pulled out the giant-sized can of hair spray. "And this. It'll keep the itching down and help dry it up, but you still might need a Benadryl."

"Hair spray?" Courtney laughed as she took the can from me. "I've used that pink stuff before, but never hair spray. Beggars can't be choosers, I guess. I don't normally get it this bad."

"You must have gotten it when we picnicked at that island while fishing yesterday," Caleb commented. "It's not like those stores you've been shopping in would have poison ivy snaking up the shelves and displays, and I haven't seen any of it around the campground."

Courtney playfully punched her husband in the shoulder. "Hey. I went on a few hikes last week. It wasn't just nonstop shopping. But you're right, I might have walked through a patch when we stopped to picnic yesterday."

"Be careful. There *is* some poison ivy on the sides of the trails," I agreed. "Poison oak and sumac too. This early in the year it can be hard to recognize the plants by the leaves. One of the other campers has a case of it as well."

"I'll be careful in the future, but for now, I'll just step out onto the porch to take my socks off and spray my legs." Courtney grimaced. "And my arms. You know, I probably should buy some Benadryl as well. I wonder if coffee will offset the drowsiness. Maybe I'll just caffeine it up and hope for the best."

Caleb leaned over and kissed the top of her head. "You go hairspray your arms and legs. I'll get the Benadryl, and an extra-large dark roast coffee for both of us. And some trail mix. And two of these blueberry muffins from the basket."

I rang up Caleb's purchases, then a couple more coffees for Drew and Bree. By the time they'd gathered up their drinks, Courtney was back smelling of hairspray and handing me the can with her thanks. I stuck it back in the bag, surprised to see Mom coming through the door as the four headed out for their equine adventure.

"You're early." I was grateful she was here, but the schedule had Mom coming in at nine, not eight.

"I'm early because you were late last night." Mom scowled and shook a finger at me. "What time did you get to bed Sassy? I didn't even hear you come in, so I know it was after midnight."

"Close to one." I told her my washing machine saga, explaining that the laundry from the cabin turnovers took longer than expected. If I couldn't get the washer fixed today, I'd be in for another long night. There were enough clean linens for the six cabins I'd be cleaning today, but I wanted the extra sets in case someone spilled coffee in bed, or if my two-week guests wanted a linen change as well.

Mom's scowl deepened. "So you got a total of three hours of sleep last night? I heard you up at four, Sassy. That's not enough sleep. Go grab a nap for the rest of the morning. I'll handle things here."

I desperately wanted a nap, but there was something else I wanted more. "I'll go to bed early tonight. And I promise I'll take a nap if I can squeeze one in this afternoon. If you can watch the store though, I want to see if I can fix that washing machine."

The scowl vanished, but it was replaced by raised eyebrows and an open-mouthed stare. "You know how to fix washing machines? Why didn't you tell me that before? That's a good skill to have."

I laughed. "The extent of my repair knowledge is an hour of watching YouTube videos. There's a good chance I might not be able to fix it. If I can't, I've got a list of repair places to call. But if I can...it would be great to have two working washers today instead of having only one and being at the mercy of some repair company's schedule."

Mom sighed. "Okay. But try to squeeze in a nap this afternoon, okay?"

I grimaced, thinking I might instead need to squeeze in a trip to Derwood to pick up washing machine parts. "No promises, Mom. But if I don't manage to get a nap, I definitely will go to bed early."

"I guess that will have to do." Mom waved a hand toward the door. "Elvis and I will hold down the fort. You go on and see if you can fix the washer."

After giving my hound a quick pat, I headed toward the laundromat, detouring to the garage to pick up a small red toolbox and a can of WD40. According to the video I had to remove the back of the washer, and I was pretty sure those screws or bolts or whatever hadn't been loosened in probably ten years.

Fifteen minutes later I'd managed to wrestle the machine away from the wall and had the back off the washer. A guest walked in with an empty laundry basket in her arms and I stared at her in dismay.

Nikki Alford. She and her husband and two children had a spiffy new RV with slide outs on both sides of the vehicle. Extended, it looked like it would be as large as an apartment inside. She'd mentioned yesterday that they wanted to come back next month if her husband Mike could manage to get another week off work. Hopefully the sad state of my laundromat wouldn't change her mind.

"Oh! You know how to fix appliances? That's so cool." Nikki laughed awkwardly. "I'm just grabbing my stuff from the dryer, then I'll be out of your hair." She walked over to one of the machines, balancing the basket on a hip as she popped the door open. "I hate having to do laundry when I get home. I'd rather spend my last morning getting things washed than deal with it after my vacation."

It made sense. "I'm sorry we were down to one washer this morning. Hope that wasn't too much of an inconvenience."

"Not at all." She gestured to a pile of wet clothes I hadn't noticed on the folding table. "I just had to take someone else's stuff out of the washer to use it. That's not your fault. I hate when people leave their stuff in the machine while they go off and do whatever. It's rude. Especially when it was clear the other washer was broken."

Now I felt worse, even though she'd said she didn't blame me for that. "I'll post some laundromat rules," I commented, thinking that I shouldn't have to remind people about common courtesy.

"The type of people who leave their clothes in the washer all morning aren't the type to pay attention to a list of posted rules." Nikki shifted the full laundry basket and closed the dryer door. "Hope to see you next month. We had a blast and can't wait to come back."

I felt so much better at her parting words, and returned my attention to the broken washing machine with a smile on my face. The smile soon faded as I watched the YouTube video once more, pausing every few seconds so I could try to copy what the woman was doing. It was difficult to see on my phone's screen, and it was clear that the washing machine she was using in the video was a different model from the one I had.

Thirty minutes and two bruised knuckles later I had a hose in one hand and a metal circular thing that had been clamping the hose onto the washing machine's water drain in the other. The hose had rotted and split. Even though that was clearly the source of the leaking water, I decided I should replace the round metal clamp thingie as well, just in case the threads were stripped so it would tighten properly.

I propped the back panel against the machine and scooted it far enough back into place that it wouldn't be in the way of my guests, but not so far that I'd need to expend unnecessary effort trying to pull it out again to install the new hose.

The pile of clothes on the folding table caught my eye just as I was getting ready to leave. Putting the hose and the clamp aside, I washed my hands in the utility sink and went over to the clothes. Rude as it was to leave clothing in the washer, whoever had done this early-morning washing was still a guest. It would be nice of me to put it all in the dryer so the camper would come back to dry clothes instead of a wet mess.

There wasn't much in the pile. Two pairs of shorts, some socks, three shirts and a sports bra. Even without taking into account the sports bra, the items were clearly women's clothing. I checked the tags and shook them out, wanting to make sure I wasn't going to inadvertently shrink a guest's clothes in the dryer. They were all machine-safe, but as I shook out a pair of shorts and a shirt, I realized why the guest had been eager to wash them before they left. Whatever they'd spilled —it looked like barbeque sauce or wine or something— hadn't come out in a single wash cycle.

I hesitated, knowing that if I put these in the dryer, the stain would set and they'd be ruined. Should I run them through a presoak and a second wash cycle? I had some detergent and stain remover in the locked utility closet.

Ultimately I decided there was a limit to my niceness. This was the busiest day of the week for me. I had guests checking out, cabins to clean, and guests checking in. And I somehow needed to squeeze in a trip to Derwood for a hose and a clamp.

And maybe squeeze in a nap.

I didn't have time to wash someone's clothes for them—especially someone who had just left them in the machine and inconvenienced another one of my guests.

So with those uncharitable thoughts, I put the wet clothes back, left the whole mess on the changing table, picked up the hose and clamp, and returned to the camp store.

CHAPTER 13

The moment I had come through the door to the camp store, Mom had stomped her foot and insisted I go take a nap, so I grabbed Elvis and reversed course back to the house where I collapsed on the sofa for a few hours of much-needed sleep.

At eleven my phone alarm woke me.

It was go-time.

Grabbing my cleaning supplies and ring of keys, I dropped Elvis off to hang out on the camp store's porch where he could watch all the action and greet anyone coming to the store. With my bucket of cleaning supplies in one hand and the mop and broom in the other, I walked to the first cabin and got to work.

Departing cabin guests always swung by the store to drop off keys on their way out. Even with a noon checkout, some guests got an early start, and that was the cabin I was heading for now. Mom would text me if anyone dropped their keys off while I was cleaning, so I'd know I was free to move on to that cabin next. Hopefully those who'd asked for a late checkout would leave a little before one since I really needed a breather between cleaning and the rush of new guests.

I got into my groove and worked my way through each cabin, cleaning, changing the sheets on the bed, and slowly washing the dirty linens in our one functioning washer. Thankfully none of the other guests came in to do their laundry and I was able to get three of the six sets cleaned, dried, folded, and stored in the linen closet. The whole time, the pile of wet—probably just damp by this time—clothing sat on the folding table.

I wondered if the guest forgot it in their rush to leave the campground. If it was still there when I fixed the washer this evening I'd go ahead and rewash the clothes, trying to get the stains out as best as I could before drying them. That way if someone contacted me about their missing clothes, I could mail them back clean and stain-free.

The clothes weren't the only thing my guests had left behind. Behind the register in the camp store was a lost-and-found box. The contents were mostly things like charging cables for phones and other devices, sunglasses, and toiletries. Once I'd found someone's keys. They must have had a spare set, because I didn't get a phone call from the guest until the following day. Last week I'd found a pair of underwear. Those I hadn't put in the lost and found box, and thankfully no one called me looking for them.

By two o'clock I'd finished with the last cabin. Damp with sweat and feeling bedraggled, I put my cleaning supplies back in the house, stopped by the laundry to shift another load of sheets from the washer to the dryer then dragged myself back to the camp store. Elvis hopped up to greet me as I climbed the steps, his long tail wagging furiously and thumping against the railing as he sniffed my legs and nudged me to beg for petting. I obliged, rubbing his long velvety ears and scratching his shoulders for a few moments before entering the store. Mom was behind the counter, sipping a cup of coffee and reading a book. She looked up as the door chimed, her smile fading when she saw me.

"Sassy, you look exhausted. Go grab a shower and take a few hours to relax. Maybe you should take another nap."

"I'm not sleepy," I told her. It wasn't exactly a lie. I *was* tired, but there was too much going on in my head to even attempt another nap. Besides, I was worried that if I got too much sleep this afternoon I'd never be able to doze off tonight, then I'd wake up tomorrow just as tired as I had this morning.

"Then take a few hours off and go for a walk, or fish off the dock, or read a book." Her worried gaze roamed over me, from my messy, sweaty hair to my damp and wrinkled pants. "Or shower, go into town, and relax with a coffee and a sandwich. Take a book with you. And Elvis."

"I don't have time," I argued, thinking that I might be able to swing a book-on-the-dock break, but not much else. "Early check-ins will start arriving in an hour, and our rush will start at four. Thursday to Saturday are our busiest days."

"I've *got* this." Her voice was stern. "I can check in the guests. Get their credit card on file. Hand over keys, activities lists, the coupons for local stores and eateries, and the FAQ sheet on campground rules and polices as well as the emergency contact number for after-hours assistance. I can tell them our store hours and what we offer, then wish them an amazing vacation. All with a smile."

She had it all down, but I still felt guilty leaving her to handle all of this while I lounged around with a book, or took a trip into town.

"Go," Mom urged. "Austin knows the routine. As soon as he gets here, he'll spring into action, prepping the RV sites and the tent camping sites. Then he can help me if it gets crazy, or he can get the firepit set up, or mow, or clean the docks and boats."

She was right. We'd established a routine over the last two months, and even though guest reservations had increased and we were close to capacity, it wasn't anything that we couldn't handle—that *Mom* couldn't handle.

"You didn't buy this place to work yourself to death," Mom scolded, repeating what she'd been telling me for the last two months. "You take the early morning shift every single day. You clean all the cabins, organize and run the activities. Even on your day off you're in the store for four hours that morning, then working late at night. Sassy, this place isn't going to fall apart if you work less than sixteen-hour days, six days a week, and another six to eight on your supposed day off."

"You deserve time off as well," I argued. "I'm not the only one working crazy hours."

Mom scowled. "Yes, you are. Did you not see me reading my book when you came in here? And I'm not reluctant to put the 'be back soon' sign on the door for thirty minutes or so. I might clock in seven hours a day, but I'm also reading or knitting or surfing the internet when it's slow. And on my Sundays off, I'm not in here for four hours in the morning and another two in the evening."

She was right, but there was a big difference between me being in my late fifties and mom in her mid-eighties. I wouldn't expect her to put in the hours I did. Plus, I was the one who'd bought this campground. We were partners, but I acutely felt the need to make it a success, to earn enough to survive. This was our first year here. This was the critical year to get the campground established and see if this was something that could provide a living income for us or not. So many small businesses failed within the first year, and I didn't want Reckless Camper Campground to be one of them.

The last was what pushed me into overworking more than any of my other excuses. I was such a type A, a driven and competitive person who was determined to succeed. After my cancer diagnosis and subsequent treatment, I'd wanted to make a change. And I had, but even though I had a heart full of good intentions, I was still me.

A leopard couldn't change its spots. I could make an effort to slow things down, but until I knew this campground was going to survive, until I had enough money to at least fix a hole in my living room ceiling, then it would be hard for me to take it easy.

Didn't mean I shouldn't try though. And I appreciated Mom for seeing me, knowing me, and calling me out when I was pushing myself too hard.

"I'll go sit on the dock with Elvis and a book," I vowed. "But I'll be back in time for the check-in rush. I do have to run in to Derwood this evening to get parts for the washing machine though, and that will be a bit of a break. Plus, I did take a nap this morning."

"Okay." Mom smiled. "I'll accept that. Baby steps."

I laughed, thinking that baby steps might be all I was capable of.

Ten minutes later I was sitting on the dock with a book and a glass of iced tea, Elvis dozing in the sunshine by my side. On the edge of dozing off myself, the sound of a truck on gravel roused both me and the hound. Elvis realized who it was before me, jumping to his feet and whacking me in the head with his wagging tail. He let out a long howl then danced, straining at the end of his leash.

He'd either recognized the truck engine sound or the scent of the vehicle and its occupant. Either way, his reaction told me who was driving around to the boat launch. It was Jake.

Sure enough, the familiar truck appeared with a trailer and the bass boat in tow. Jake expertly maneuvered the vehicle, backing the trailer down the ramp and putting it in park when the water came up to the bottom of the boat.

I stood, unhooking Elvis when I saw Jake get out of the truck so the hound could race over to greet him.

"You're getting a late start," I called out as I made my way over to him, my pace slower than my hound's.

Jake bent over to pet the enthusiastic Elvis, then smiled up at me. "I know. Doubt I'll catch anything this time of day, but a few hours on the water is still better than none at all."

I grinned, thinking that Mom would absolutely agree with him. "Busy morning?"

He nodded. "Had to do some police work to help Sean and Oliver, then I needed to be home for a feed delivery at eleven."

"Door Dash?" I hadn't thought they delivered out here, but I couldn't think of any other food delivery Jake might need at eleven in the morning.

He laughed. "Feed, not food. The horses gotta eat, you know? I work with the co-op out of Derwood to put together a special grain mix for my senior guys, and they deliver the bags once a month. I need to be there to help unload and get the grain stored in the feed room."

"Your horses get a gourmet blend of grains?" I teased. "I'm guessing they also have organic alfalfa bales? Weekly massages? Heated stalls?"

"I don't have the money for all that, or trust me, I'd make it happen. The feed isn't exactly gourmet, but older horses often have special needs. Indy has trouble keeping weight on and needs a high protein and high fat mix. Nova's teeth are pretty worn, so he needs flaked feed instead of pellets, and I need to add water and applesauce to turn it into easy-to-chew mush. Hershey has a metabolic issue and can't have much fresh grass, especially this time of year, so he gets hay extender pellets to get him the extra calories without the extra sugar. And they all need daily supplements for joint issues."

Wow. Taking care of horses was a whole lot more complicated than I'd ever thought. Although caring for retired, older horses was probably more work than caring for the younger ones. Just like people, I guessed. Mom and I had more health concerns, more medicines and supplements, than either of us had needed in our youth.

"Glad you're at least getting in a few hours on the water," I commented. "How did the police-work go this morning? Is Scat still in custody? Did he get charged for the murder, or just the trespass and attempted vandalism?"

Jake rolled his eyes, then spoke as he began to unhook his boat. "I should probably keep my mouth shut and not comment, but I'm sure Lottie will be calling you today and telling you stuff that even I don't know about. Scat was released on his own recognizance this morning. He's facing the trespass and intent charges in regards to vandalism, but between you and me, I think the county isn't going to push it. He'll probably get a PBJ."

I nodded, recognizing the term as "probation before judgement." Basically if Scat kept his nose clean and satisfied any court requirements, the charges wouldn't officially go on his record, but they would resurface if he got arrested and charged with anything else in the future.

"So...no murder charges?" I was prying, but Reckless was a town where the normal secrecy around law enforcement actions didn't seem to apply.

"I'm not saying they won't come in the future, but things don't add up for Scat being the murderer. At least, not at this time. We've needed to be careful and have our ducks in a row when we charge someone, otherwise it sets us back or can even derail the investigation and prosecution entirely."

I nodded, thinking about all the crime shows Mom and I had watched. It made sense. Charge someone for the thing you had solid evidence on, use that as a chance to get them into the station for questioning, then bide your time and cast your net. Step by step. It was like working a puzzle, putting different sections together then seeing where they connected until it was all filled in.

"I don't think he did it," I said, realizing that Jake probably didn't care one bit about my opinion on the investigation. "He confessed to the trespass and attempted vandalism readily, but stuck to his claims of innocence on the murder. Plus, the timeline doesn't work out. Neither does the motive in my opinion."

Jake waded through the water to the other side of the trailer, unhooking the latches. "One thing that did come out of this is that Scat inadvertently provided an alibi for Danielle. He saw the inspector alive and sound at the time Danielle was on her way to town to help rescue Squeakers. He allowed us to narrow down the time of death, and rule out our main suspect." Jake glanced up at me. "I'm glad. I didn't like thinking Danielle might have killed someone. It didn't sit right with me."

I frowned, thinking. "That cuts things kinda close though. The killer must have struck soon after Wilber Kendricks chased Scat off the field. Maybe Scat saw something."

"Maybe. Maybe not." Jake gave me an enigmatic smile before easing his boat off the trailer and tying it to a post. "I'm surprised to see you sitting out on the dock this afternoon. Isn't Thursday your turnover day?"

It was my turn to roll my eyes. "Yes, but Mom insisted I take a break. I was up early handling checkouts, then cleaning cabins, so she kicked me out and told me to relax. I'm having an ulcer over not being there. I think I might just chill for another hour, then get back to the store before the rush starts."

"Workaholic," Jake teased.

It was the truth.

"Have fun fishing," I told Jake. Then I watched as he pulled the truck and trailer away to the parking area. Elvis and I walked back to the dock and relaxed. A few minutes later Jake came back, untied his boat, and with a wave headed out to fish. I watched him make his way out onto the lake, thinking about the food needs of elderly horses.

The co-op. Marsha Kendricks, Wilber Kendricks's ex-wife, worked there. In Derwood—the town I'd be driving to late this afternoon to buy a new hose and clamp for the washing machine.

Maybe I'd take a quick detour to the co-op, pick up some dog food, and have a chat with Marsha Kendricks.

CHAPTER 14

$\mathcal{B}$y four o'clock we had a line out the camp store's door. The parking lot was full of cars, trucks, campers, and RVs. In spite of the wait, my new guests were patient and in a good mood, getting cups of coffee, browsing the store, and chatting with others as they waited for their turn to check in. I was glad I hadn't let Mom handle it all solo since things definitely went smoother and faster with two of us helping the guests. Austin had popped in right at four, giving me a thumb's up to indicate that all the tent and camper sites were clean and ready for the new arrivals. Then he shifted focus, helping guests find their locations and assisting anyone who needed help pounding in tent stakes, or leveling their campers and hooking up to shore power and water.

By five thirty all our guests had arrived and were busy settling in. I glanced at my watch, calculated the drive to Derwood, then turned to Mom.

"Do you mind if I run out for an hour or so?" I asked. "Austin is making the rounds among the guests. At this point

I think all we'll get in the store is people who are picking up milk or something they forgot to pack."

"Go." She waved at the door. "I might put the sign on the door and run to the house around six or seven for a bite to eat, but other than that, I'm fine. Are you taking Elvis?"

I felt a little guilty that Elvis hadn't had more than a quick walk in the morning and some lazy time on the dock, but Thursdays were always like this. I knew the hound had enjoyed his time on the porch, greeting people as they came and went. Still, I felt like I should pay more attention to him.

"I'm heading into Derwood to get the parts for the washing machine and to make a quick stop at the co-op, but I think he'd like a ride."

Elvis lifted his head, his ears coming forward and his droopy eyes focused on me at the word "ride." He loved being in the car, smelling all the scents that came through the partially open window. And he loved that I usually stopped somewhere and got a treat for both of us.

"The co-op?" Mom's puzzled expression suddenly cleared. "Oh. Going to chat with Marsha Kendricks, are you?"

"If she's in. If not, I'll just pick up a bag of dog food and head back."

"Get some birdseed while you're there," Mom said. "The squirrels keep getting into the feeder by the dock and we're almost out."

I had mixed feelings about that bird feeder—and the squirrels. The birds coming to eat were pretty and guests seemed to like them, but attracting them meant there was more poop to pressure wash off the dock. The squirrels could be a nuisance, and I also worried the feeder would attract animals like racoons that I especially didn't want deciding our campground was an all-they-could-eat buffet of camper food. But Mom liked to sit out and watch the birds, so I left the feeder up and had Austin fill it a couple of times each week.

Promising I'd pick up birdseed, I untied Elvis and headed for my SUV. The hound claimed shotgun, and had his nose pressed to the window opening as we made our way down the drive, sniffing away.

It was thirty minutes to Derwood and the big-box home improvement store. They were dog-friendly, so Elvis trotted by my side at the end of a leash as we went up and down several aisles looking for the appliance parts. Thankfully an employee finally showed up to help me locate the correct size hose and clamp. I picked up a box-cutter while I was there so I could trim the new hose to size, and also bought grout cleaner for the campground showers. Our main shopping completed, I pulled the address for the co-op up on Google Maps and let my phone navigate me to the other side of Derwood.

Pulling in where my phone told me to turn, I drove past grain silos, a warehouse where I assumed they bagged the feed, and loading docks, to park in front of a small one-story building. Inside the store were several aisles with horse halters, mineral blocks, and assorted poultry supplies. Behind the counter was a huge white board with different feed mixes listed alongside their prices.

A slim man in his mid-twenties with a baseball cap and a full dark beard was at the computer. My heart sank, as I realized I'd probably be leaving with a bag of dog food and one of birdseed, and no answers.

He glanced up at me and smiled. "Can I help you find something? We're getting ready to close, but I can call over to the loading docks if you're picking up feed and ask them to wait."

"Dog food and birdseed," I told him.

He shifted to the side and looked out the window at my

SUV, his smile broadening. "Is that a bloodhound? What a gorgeous boy."

"His name is Elvis." I liked this man. Anyone who complimented my dog definitely scored points in my book.

"What do you feed him?" he asked. "We don't bag the dog food here, but we carry several brands formulated for hunting breeds. Lamb and chickpea. Salmon and sweet potato. Venison and lentils. They're all high-protein for working dogs."

"Uhh, what do you recommend?" I didn't feed Elvis cheap generic food, but I did tend to just grab a forty-pound bag of name-brand stuff at the grocery store and I wasn't really sure what was in it.

"If he's got problems with allergies and ear infections, then you might want to try the salmon and sweet potato. Honestly they're all high quality. It really depends on your dog's preference. Some are picky."

I laughed. "Elvis is not picky. He eats anything—and I mean anything. We have to be careful what we leave out because he can get up on the counters. And we've got locks on the garbage can lids."

He shook his head and made a "tsk" noise. "Typical hound. I'd suggest getting a couple different five-pound bags and see which he prefers before shelling out for fifty pounds of food, though. Even garbage-eating hounds might up and decide they don't like lamb or something."

I glanced out at Elvis who had his head out the passenger side window, slobbering down the side of the glass. "Then I'll go with a bag of the salmon, and another of the venison. I know he likes venison."

He typed something into the computer. "And ten pounds of songbird seed?"

"That sounds perfect." I walked up to the counter, digging in my purse for my wallet.

The man finished typing, picked up the phone and dialed a number. He relayed to someone at the other end that I'd be coming by to get an order, then told me the total.

I nearly fainted. Evidently high quality, performance dog food was about double the cost of the stuff I'd been buying at the grocery store. For that price, Elvis better have the glossiest coat and best health of his life.

"I was hoping to run into Marsha Kendricks," I said as I swiped my debit card. "Danielle Pouliette gave me her name when she recommended I come here for dog food."

It was a bit of a lie. Danielle had mentioned Marsha worked at the co-op, but she hadn't pointed me here to get food for Elvis.

"Marsha's out at the loading docks right now putting together tomorrow's deliveries," the man said. "Just ask for her when you pick up your dog food and birdseed. And tell Danielle that Steele from over at the co-op said hi. She's good people. And I'm sorry she's going through all this trouble with her crop. I'm four-twenty friendly myself and know lots of people who support her and the new laws."

I had no idea what four-twenty friendly was, but I told Steele I'd relay his message, got my receipt, and left. Elvis was very excited to see me as I climbed back into the SUV because like a typical dog, he'd felt I'd been gone *forever*, and might never have come back. The hound grew more excited as we pulled around to the loading docks, sticking his head out the window and letting out a mournful howl to announce our arrival to the employees.

"A bloodhound!" a young man with a blond ponytail and tattooed arms called out before turning around to look behind him. "Bob! Marsha! Come see this hound!"

By the time I was out of my vehicle, receipt in hand, three people were at my passenger side window, making a huge fuss over Elvis. He was reveling in the attention, tail whacking my dash and seat. His butt wiggled as he danced back and forth, and he panted, slobbering all over the people who were petting him and telling him he was a good boy.

The dog food at the co-op might be expensive, but I was now a loyal customer because the employees seemed to love my dog just as much as I did.

"I know you all are getting ready to close, but I'm picking up some dog food and birdseed." I handed my receipt to the other man, who I assumed was Bob.

He reluctantly gave Elvis another pat, then took my receipt, jumping back up onto the loading dock and into the warehouse.

I smiled at the woman. "Are you Marsha Kendricks? Danielle Pouliette mentioned your name to me."

She nodded. "That's me. How's Danielle holding up? I hear she's had some trouble over at her farm."

Marsha said this with a certain wariness that told me she knew about the murder, and more importantly, knew *who* was murdered. It made sense. I was sure the police had done the same research my mother had, although probably a lot quicker, and come by to talk to Marsha.

"Danielle's doing okay. I was wondering if I could ask you a few questions, though. I was there...that day, and I've been trying to help her out as best as I can. She was a suspect, you know."

Marsha's eyes widened. "No. I didn't realize that." She turned to the other man. "Robby, you scat. Let me speak with this lady in private a minute or two, okay?"

"Sure Marsha." Robby rubbed Elvis's ears, then went back into the warehouse.

"Robby and Bob?" I laughed, thinking it was easier than having two Bobs working at the co-op.

"Robert's a popular name in Derwood." Marsha chuckled, then her expression sobered. "I guess everyone's made the connection between Wilber and me. I should have changed my name after the divorce, but we had a child, and then after decades had passed, it didn't seem worth the bother or the money, so I stayed Kendricks. Now I'm thinking I should have bothered."

"I'm so sorry. It must be horrible to have all this dredged up after so much time," I said in sympathy.

"It is. I should have known even after all these years Wil would find a way to still mess with me. He screwed me over when we were eighteen, and he's still screwing me over now, even from beyond the grave."

I winced, uncomfortable with her strong feelings toward her ex-husband. Maybe she *had* murdered him. I'd assumed too much water had passed under the bridge for her to lash out with violence now, but perhaps he'd continued to do little things to her over the decades, and those things had added up. Everyone had their breaking point. It could be that Marsha had reached hers and snapped.

But then why be so vocal about her feelings? If she'd killed her ex, surely she'd be smart enough to act like with the passage of time, she just didn't care anymore.

Marsha sighed and ran a hand through her hair. "Sorry. It's just been a stressful week. I haven't seen Wilber since our daughter's college graduation. I was shocked when the police showed up a few days ago to tell me he was dead."

"So your marriage was…rocky?" I asked.

"Not in the beginning. I mean, we argued a lot, and that should have been a red flag, but we dated all through high school. Neither of us knew any different. Wasn't like either of our parents had a good marriage to base our expectations on."

"You got married right out of high school and moved to Roanoke?"

She nodded. "His cousin got him a job with the county

government, so we had some decent money starting out. We weren't rich or anything, but we could afford an apartment and a car. I got a job at a nearby hardware store close enough to home that I could walk to and from work until we saved enough for a second car. Even after Chloe was born, we did okay."

"What happened to cause the divorce?" I asked.

She shrugged. "Lots of little things. He worked as a health inspector and was gone long hours, traveling all around the county. I was alone a lot and the care for Chloe fell solely on my shoulders. When he was home, we either ignored each other or argued about stupid stuff. We didn't really have anything solid to keep our marriage together and I think eventually we would have split anyway, but the breaking point came for me when he got the transfer from health inspection into a state job doing liquor inspections. He was never home. Then I found the money one night in his dresser drawers and confronted him about it."

"Money?" My mouth dropped open, wondering where all this was going.

"He never fessed up, but I think he was taking kickbacks or blackmailing people. It was cash. Lots of twenties. And other than drug dealing, I couldn't see any other reason for him to have a few thousand in twenties stuffed under his socks."

I frowned. "Are you sure it wasn't drugs?" It would be a horrible irony for the man who was in charge of inspecting cannabis facilities for the state to be a drug dealer on the side.

She shook her head. "I turned that apartment upside down when I found the money. There was no scale, no baggies, no drugs, no weapons. I had a cousin who got popped for dealing when I was in high school, so I know what kind of stuff dealers have. After Wil got home one night, I even searched his car and found nothing. I figured someone who was doing liquor inspections for bars and restaurants and places selling beer and wine would be in an ideal position to accept bribes for looking the other way on a violation. Or for pressuring someone into paying blackmail to avoid being accused of something they weren't doing. And Wilber was just the sort of man who'd do that. He didn't care about anyone but himself. Not me outside of sex and companionship. Not Chloe either, besides the fact that he was proud of her as a child he'd fathered."

"Did you call the police? Or whatever agency handles liquor licensing to report that one of their inspectors was on the take?" I asked.

She looked down at the ground. "No. I didn't have anything but suspicions and the money, and I didn't think anyone would believe me. But I wasn't about to stick around and be that woman whose husband goes to jail. Or risk myself and Chloe because he wanted to be a criminal. I told him I'd keep my mouth shut if he gave me five hundred and the car, and let me leave with Chloe. He agreed so I packed and we left that night. Came back to Derwood. Stayed with my parents until I could get on my feet again. Chloe and I did without a lot of things, but we had a roof over our heads, food on the table, and we didn't have to worry about the cops breaking in our door one night."

Well, *that* expanded the pool of suspects considerably. Wilber could have pissed off the wrong person with his illegal activities. Or even stepped on the toes of the mob. I had no idea if the Mafia were active in Roanoke and had no experience with them outside of watching *The Godfather* and a few television series, but I got the feeling they might be more than a little irked at someone shaking down businesses in their territory—especially if Wilber wasn't giving them a cut. I could absolutely see Tony Soprano sending one of his guys to follow and "take care of" Wilber Kendricks.

"What was Wilber's inspection territory back then?" I wondered, not sure how many businesses one health inspector, or even alcohol inspector, was expected to cover.

"When he was a health inspector, it was Roanoke County, but he had assigned businesses because the number of restaurants and bars in the area is more than one person can manage. He covered almost the whole county when he moved to liquor inspections for the state."

Marsha looked over my shoulder and I turned to see Bob with a cart that held several bags of dog food and one of birdseed. He looked like he'd been standing there a while, waiting for us to finish talking.

"I should let you get back to work," I said, feeling a little guilty that I was keeping these people from finishing up and going home for the day. "Thanks for answering my questions."

"No problem." She waved Bob over. "I didn't realize the police were eyeing Danielle for this. She's good people. And I support what she's doing. It's hard to keep a farm going these days. Farmers have to be creative, and she worked really hard to get that pot contract."

"You talking about Danielle Pouliette?" Bob said as he loaded the bags into the back of my SUV. "I'm psyched to buy local weed that isn't from some dude with a grow lamp in his basement. She's got some good strains too."

Marsha rolled her eyes. "All the stoners have come out of the closet now that it's legal. It's not my thing, but I'm glad there's safe, tested, and consistent product for people who partake. I figure it can't be any worse than alcohol."

I didn't know enough to either agree or disagree with that statement, so I mumbled something noncommittal, thanked Marsha and Bob, and headed home.

As I drove, Elvis sniffed the passing smells with half his nose out the window, and I thought about liquor inspections. What sort of things could get a business in trouble with the licensing board? Selling to underage individuals, probably, but what else? Those alcohol licenses couldn't be super easy to come by. Was there a waiting list? A set number of alcohol licenses per county? An endless amount of hoops to jump through and criteria to meet? I was sure the license wasn't cheap to acquire, but was there an annual fee? If someone had a bar and lost their ability to serve alcohol, they'd pretty much be out of business, so I could see where a dirty inspector could use his power to make some illegal money on the side.

I was beginning to think Wilber Kendricks's death wasn't something to be terribly sad over. According to Marsha, he'd been a real jerk. But I didn't want to just take an ex-wife's opinion as the whole truth. Maybe there was some other reason for Wilber to have that money in his sock drawer decades ago. Surely if he'd been taking kickbacks and squeezing businesses, *someone* would have complained? Surely there would have been an investigation, and he would have been fired, not promoted to be a cannabis inspector in a newly-formed state-level agency? Maybe Marsha was still harboring a grudge from their unhappy marriage and her theories about her ex's illegal activities were wrong.

Yes, the man had shifty-looking eyes in his high school photo, but a bad photograph at eighteen wasn't a solid basis to make a moral judgment on.

CHAPTER 15

*I*t was still light out when I got back to the campground, so I dropped Elvis off with Mom at the camp store and went to the laundromat with the replacement parts and my toolbox, texting Austin on my way to ask if he could come over and give me a hand.

The pile of clothes was gone from the folding table. The guest must have returned to retrieve their clothing, or someone had stolen it. Either way I was taking it as a good omen, a weird sign that my amateur repair efforts might actually be a success.

Setting my tools and parts on the table, I hauled the washing machine away from the wall, putting the back panel aside. Then I took out the old hose and marked the length on the new one, giving myself an inch extra. I could always trim the excess hose off if needed, but there was no putting it back on if I cut it too short.

Once the hose was cut, I pulled out my phone and again watched the YouTube video, pausing it as I followed the instructions on installing the new hose and tightening the circular clamp to secure it to the drain outlet on the washer tub.

"Did you need me, Miss Sassy? Whoa! Look at you, fixing appliances."

I scowled up at Austin, not appreciating his incredulous tone. "It's the twenty-first century. Women fix things. We run corporations. We even get out of the kitchen with our shoes on while not pregnant on occasion."

He eyed me in confusion. "Well, yeah. Of course. But weren't you a marketing person or something before you bought the campground? And the hole is still in your living room ceiling, so I just figured you weren't a fix-it kind of person. Didn't mean to offend you or anything."

Maybe the next thing I Googled should be how to repair drywall. I was willing to bet there was a YouTube video for that as well.

"No offense taken." I waved the apology away. "I'm just grumpy because I don't know what I'm doing and I'm worried that after all this effort, the stupid thing is still going to leak."

"Only one way to find out," Austin announced cheerfully. "What do you need my help with?"

"I need to push the washing machine partially back, connect the other end of this hose to the PVC drainpipe, then push the machine completely back so it's flush with the other one. Then I need to make sure it's level." I eyed him. "That sounded like a two-person job to me."

It also sounded like a job that required someone with more strength than I had. If the machine wasn't level, Austin would need to tilt a corner up while I reached under and adjusted the feet. I might not know much about appliances, but I knew from experience that a non-level washer would walk itself across the floor in the spin cycle, and that eventually the motor might burn out. I didn't want my repair job to end with my having to replace the washer in a month or two.

Austin nodded. "I can help with that. We should probably run a wash cycle when we're done to make sure everything is okay."

Of course, I'd run a test cycle. I was mostly worried that after all this work the hose would pop free and spew water everywhere, or I'd find out that the tub was also leaking, or that one of the more technical repairs was needed.

I said a quick prayer that my repair would pass the test. God probably had more important things to do than intervene with my appliance woes, but I figured it wouldn't hurt to ask for some divine assistance.

Austin helped me ease the machine back into place, then I stood on the step stool and leaned precariously over the washer to insert the new hose into the PVC drainpipe. The extra inch on the hose thankfully didn't seem to matter, because I really didn't want to have to haul the washer out again. We wiggled it all the way back, then I got up on the step stool once more to check that the hose hadn't popped out of place during the movement. After checking that, I pulled the small level from the toolbox. The poured concrete floor of the laundromat seemed pretty flat to me, but we ended up needing to make a few adjustments to get the washer level.

With another silent prayer, I turned the washer on and stood back. It probably wasn't the best use of Austin's time standing in the laundromat staring at a washing machine in case water started pouring everywhere, but I wanted him nearby if disaster struck.

I barely breathed for fifteen minutes as I watched the washer with rapt attention. No water appeared, but I held off on any jubilation until it had finished its spin cycle and had come to a slow stop.

"Woohoo!" I jumped, pumping my fist in the air. Then I gave Austin a high five.

"Nice work, Miss Sassy," he said, ending the high five with some complicated elbow-fist-palm smack that I followed with difficulty.

I'd done it. I'd repaired the washer and saved myself a few hundred dollars in the process. I should be only cautiously optimistic, because there was still a good chance the ancient appliance would break again within the next few days or weeks or months, but I couldn't help my giddy excitement. I'd fixed a washing machine. Fixed it.

Maybe I could fix that hole in the living room ceiling as well? Getting rid of that embarrassing blue tarp was now something that might actually happen in the next week or so. I was going to start watching drywall repair videos.

But not now. I was exhausted and hungry, and tomorrow was a busy day at the campground. Further repair efforts would need to at least wait for the weekend, or possibly until my day off next Tuesday.

* * *

"Mafia?" Mom's eyes widened.

I nodded, swallowing the mouthful of the leftover chili that was my dinner tonight. "I don't know for sure if the Mafia is involved, but it sounds like Wilber Kendricks might have been taking bribes and blackmailing the businesses he was supposed to be inspecting."

Mom glanced at the door nervously, as if she expected suited mobsters carrying tommy guns to burst into our house at any moment. "Sassy, if you really think that inspector died because of a mob hit, then you need to stay out of this investigation. There's being curious and trying to help a friend, and then there's putting yourself in danger. Let the police deal with gangsters."

"Trust me, I don't want to get in the middle of any organized crime business," I assured her. "But that theory seems kind of a stretch, don't you think? Outside of the movies, does that stuff really happen? I just can't imagine the Mafia finding enough business in Roanoke, or these small Virginia mountain towns, to profitably operate."

"There's gangs other than the Mafia, and it seems like there's drugs everywhere nowadays," Mom pointed out. "If Wilber Kendricks was doing shady stuff under the cover of his inspection job, then he might have decided to branch out into drugs. His wife left him a long time ago, and she said they didn't exactly keep in touch, so she'd have no idea what the man was involved with in recent years."

"True." I took another bite of chili and thought for a bit. "There's so much I'm unfamiliar with surrounding this murder, and not just the possible organized crime angle either. I don't know anything about alcohol inspections or what sort of things might be used as leverage to demand payoff from a bar owner. I only know minimal stuff about how the cannabis licensing, distribution, and inspection works in the state. Honestly, I barely know anything about pot at all. Suddenly it seems like tons of people were secret marijuana users and are now open about their habit, while I'm clueless about it all. Smoking, vaping, gummies, and oils? Different strains and their recreational and medical use? And 'four-twenty friendly,' whatever the heck that is?"

"Four twenty refers to twenty minutes after four in the afternoon," Mom said. "I believe it originated because it was the time when high school students were out of classes for the day and gathered to smoke weed together. 'Four-twenty friendly' means someone either enjoys marijuana themselves or is accepting of those who do."

I turned to stare at her. "How do you know this stuff? How come you know pot slang, and I don't?"

"I'm curious, just like you, only I tend to be curious about different things. Plus, I've always been a fan of Willie Nelson and he's a strong advocate for the legalization of marijuana."

"You like country music?" All I'd ever heard my mom listen to over the years was what was commonly called "yacht rock".

"Actually, I do like Willie's music. But besides that, I was reading an article one day, decided to look something up, and I ended up going down a rabbit hole of marijuana research. It was very interesting, Sassy. Did you know cannabis is one of the oldest crops, having been cultivated for over twelve thousand years? George Washington grew it at Mount Vernon—although I don't know if he actually smoked it or not. Hemp is a very useful fiber, so he may not have been using the plants for a recreational high."

Even after all these years, there were still moments where my mother truly surprised me. "No, I did not know that. Mom...have you ever...did you ever smoke pot?"

"Pfft." Mom waved a hand dismissively. "You couldn't live through the sixties and seventies without at least getting a contact high off second-hand pot smoke. Half the parties your father and I went to had someone passing a joint around in the basement. Thankfully by the eighties when people started doing lines of cocaine, your father and I were past the stage of attending those sorts of parties. Alcohol and pot and loud music had become card games or barbeques with the kids in attendance at that point."

I noticed she didn't exactly answer my question, but I didn't press her. There were things that people wanted to keep private, and just because I was her daughter, she was under no obligation to tell me about any of the activities Mom and Dad might have done in their youth.

She laughed. "Did you know your father once bought me a set of marijuana leaf earrings from a stand at a county fair? They were silver with turquoise chips and really pretty. He had no idea, of course."

"Wait…I remember those earrings. Those were *pot* leaves? I thought they were some kind of fern or something." Like my father, I evidently had no idea either.

"Oh, they were marijuana leaves all right. Of course I wore them anyway. Half the people at bridge night were giving me funny looks, but I acted clueless, so they didn't say anything. Then there was the time your father bought me a roach clip with feathers hanging from it as a hair ornament."

"That was a barrette!" I protested. "He bought me one too! I used to wear it to school."

Mom laughed. "Lots of people wore them as barrettes, but that pincher-clip you used to secure it to your hair? It's also to hold your joint so you can smoke it all the way down and not burn your fingers."

I stared at her, open-mouthed. "You let me go to school with drug paraphernalia in my hair? Mom!"

"Well, they *were* pretty," she argued. "And it wasn't like anyone would think you were really smoking pot at nine years old with your pastel button-down shirts and matching pink pants. I figured everyone should wear feathers in their hair, regardless if they'd need to use their barrette later to hold a joint or not."

"Good grief. Now I know who to go to with all my questions about marijuana," I teased her, still appalled that I'd been prancing around grade school with a roach clip in my hair. Good thing Dad had never come home with a bong for Mom to put my milk in for school lunches.

"Do you have equal knowledge about liquor inspections in the State of Virginia? Regulations concerning licensing of bars?" I asked.

"No, I don't, but you know who might?" Mom smiled. "The owner of the Twelve Gauge, that's who. I'm thinking we need to make a trip there and ask him all about his business. If we hurry, we might still make it in time for the trivia contest tonight."

I laughed. "We can't leave the campground unattended on a Thursday night to go to a sketchy bar to play trivia. And I think they'll be too busy at night for us to grill the owner or manager. Maybe we can sneak out Saturday afternoon. Let's see what time they open. They can't be too busy then, and by Saturday afternoon our guests will mostly be settled in and enjoying their day. We can leave Austin in charge, and dash out for an hour or so."

"It's a date, although I do want to catch trivia night there sometime. Maybe this winter when we're closed for the season?"

I wasn't sure we'd be able to afford completely closing for the season. I couldn't imagine much in the way of tent or camper spot rentals when there was snow on the ground, but I was seriously considering running the numbers and seeing if we could do cabin rentals. We would need to bring in enough money to cover clearing snow around the cabins, plus heating them as well as heating the communal bathrooms, the laundry, and the game room. Would demand be sufficient to even bother? I hated the idea of having four to five months with zero income, but there was no sense spending time and money if only a handful of people were willing to brave the cold and the snow. And what would they do? Hiking wasn't out of the question, but no one was going to be taking canoes and kayaks out to fish on a half-frozen lake. There was a small ski resort ten miles away, but I'd be competing with closer hotels that had far more amenities for those guests.

Once more I thought of the checking account balance,

and sighed. We needed to have enough of a cushion to poten-tially go four to five months with no revenue. That meant I needed to be frugal and cut corners. And I needed to get creative about how I could turn those potentially zero income months into months with enough income to at least cover the mortgage, the utilities, and our food.

"They're open at noon." Mom turned her phone around so I could see that she'd pulled up the Twelve Gauge's hours of operation. "*And* they have a lunch menu. It's mostly fried stuff, but I'm not a woman to turn up my nose at a plate of jalapeño poppers."

Me neither. I laughed, scooping some more chili onto my spoon. "Then we're sneaking out Saturday afternoon for lunch at the Twelve Gauge."

Mom grinned, putting her phone down. "Lunch Saturday, and then maybe trivia night in a few months."

If Mom really wanted to go to trivia night this badly, then I'd make it happen. The high school kids would be out for summer soon. Maybe I could pay Austin and a friend of his to watch the campground late Thursday while Mom and I kicked butt at trivia. We wouldn't have to necessarily wait until winter when the campground was closed.

Life was short. And I needed to trust someone else to hold down the fort while I had some fun with my mother. She was eighty-five, after all, and I'd had a serious health scare recently.

Sometime in the next month, we were definitely going to play trivia at the Twelve Gauge.

After dinner I took Elvis for a walk, and decided to make a quick phone call.

Lottie picked up on the second ring.

"Hey, Mom and I are going over to the Twelve Gauge Saturday afternoon, and I wondered if you'd mind babysitting the campground with Austin for two or three hours while we're gone."

I knew I'd feel a lot better about Mom and I both being gone if someone besides my teenaged employee was here to help out.

"The Twelve Gauge? Seriously?" She snorted. "Why are you going there? It's dead on a Saturday afternoon. No bar fights. No stabbings. No illegal gambling in the back room."

Good. I'd picked the perfect day and time then.

"It's a long story," I explained. "Basically, Wilber Kendricks's ex-wife said she thought he was taking kickbacks and blackmailing bars and restaurants when he was a liquor inspector. I want to find out what sort of things could get a bar in trouble enough that they might be willing to pay someone off."

Lottie snorted. "And you decided to go to the Twelve Gauge with these questions rather than a respectable establishment like the Chat-n-Chew?"

She had a point.

"I figured if someone wanted to take payoffs, they'd target places like the Twelve Gauge," I explained. I felt a bad disparaging a place I'd never been to, but I'd been told it was a dive. I'd been told they ran illegal gambling in a back room, and that some rather dicey people frequented there. If there was a place that was doing sketchy stuff that might put them at odds with the regulations surrounding their liquor license, it was more likely an establishment like the Twelve Gauge.

"So that's why you're taking your *mother* there?" Lottie squeaked.

"She's been dying to go ever since she found out about trivia night." I sighed. "Mom's eccentric. The reputation there is more of an attraction than a deterrent to her. We can't get away Thursday nights for trivia, so this is kind of a compromise. Plus, I figured I can kill two birds with one stone."

"If you guys decide to go one Thursday night, then you better take me," Lottie insisted. "I'm not staying behind while you and your mom have all the fun."

Fun. Potential stabbings aside.

"I promise I'll bring you next time. It might not be until this winter though, during our off season. Or until I can convince someone over the age of eighteen to watch the campground. Check-in is Thursday, and if someone has a problem with their hookups, or the ceiling fans in the cabins, or has a disagreement with a neighbor who set up their tent too close, then it's going to happen Thursday night."

I was rambling, probably because the idea of Thursday night at the Twelve Gauge scared me.

"It's no problem. I'll come over and watch the campground for you tomorrow afternoon, but only if you tell me everything that happened when you get back," Lottie said.

"Of course I will." I was *so* relieved that Austin wouldn't be here alone, even though we'd probably only be gone a few hours.

"And I'm definitely taking that rain check on a future trip," Lottie warned. "I haven't been there in ages, and there's no way I'll go alone. It's not like Scotty is ever going to go with me. Dive bars aren't his thing. So it'll have to be you and me. And your mom. I'll bet she kicks butt at trivia."

She probably *would* kick butt at trivia. And although I had hoped this wouldn't be a regular thing, between Mom and Lottie, I might end up being a Twelve Gauge regular.

"Okay. It's a deal. Maybe we can go next Saturday around lunch time," I offered, thinking that might be safer for all of us, trivia contest aside.

"I don't think the Twelve Gauge is very fun on a Saturday afternoon," Lottie complained.

"That's what I'm hoping for," I told her.

"I mean, that's probably the perfect time to take your

eighty-five-year-old mother, but I'm looking for a little more action," Lottie pointed out, as if she hadn't met my mother at all. "There will be the usual day-drinkers propping up the bar, but the likelihood of a knife fight or a raid for illegal gambling is less."

"Thanks for that reassurance," I drawled.

"I'd actually like to see a brawl, or a raid, or a knife fight," Lottie went on. "From a distance, of course."

"How about from three blocks over?" That was the closest I wanted to be to a brawl, a raid, or a knife fight.

Lottie laughed. "I'll compromise. How about we go next Tuesday night? It shouldn't be too crazy, and that's supposed to be your day off anyway. I know you're still working mornings and evenings, so it'll be good for you to actually extend your free time to more than a few hours in town getting lunch and reading a book."

"Tuesday it is. Thanks for helping me out, and I'll see you tomorrow." I disconnected the call, then walked Elvis back to the house, ready to call it an early night and go to bed.

CHAPTER 16

eckless Neighbors App:
Traffic alert: A reminder that Main Street will be closed between nine and ten this Saturday morning for the Reckless Youth Club Stick-Horse Race. Ten-year-old MarySue Bowman is currently the odds-on favorite at 2-1. Racing forms available at the Community Center. Turn them in with your bet/donation at the drop box in Community Center or prior to post time at the starting gate.

Thankfully there were no emergencies that disrupted my sleep, so I was up at four, refreshed and ready for the fun that came with new guests on their first day of vacation as well as the activities I'd planned for tonight's bonfire.

I quickly showered, brushed my teeth, and threw on my clothes, then I let Elvis take a potty break before stopping by the camp store to get the coffee urns percolating. While the coffee brewed, I took Elvis for a longer walk, trying to not wake any of my guests with either noise or my flashlight. It was a good opportunity to see who else in the campground was an early riser and judge how busy I'd be each morning.

All the tents, cabins, and campers were dark, so when

Elvis and I got back to the store, I took my time organizing the shelves and the sign-up list for food orders, then relaxed with a cup of fresh coffee and a day-old pastry. Elvis had some of his new salmon and sweet potato dog food. He seemed to really enjoy it, but I wasn't crazy about the fishy odor on his breath after he'd eaten breakfast. Hopefully the venison wouldn't be as stinky.

I went ahead and flipped the sign to "Open" at five thirty, even though Flora wouldn't arrive for another half an hour with fresh pastries and the handful of food orders that had been placed yesterday at check-in. As I glanced out over the campground I saw a number of people stirring in the dim light of dawn. A few were already making their way to the store, drawn like moths to the golden glow coming from the windows.

I sold coffee and rented three kayaks to people who weren't about to wait even one day before fishing on the lake. Flora arrived just as the rush was beginning to start. I put the box of food orders behind the counter, making sure it was out of Elvis's reach, then continued to ring up sales as Flora stocked the bags of coffee as well as the pastry case and the various foods that went in the refrigerator.

A little after seven Bree came in, still in her pajamas and yawning as she poured two coffees.

"How was the horseback riding yesterday?" I asked as I rang up her coffees.

"Amazing." She chuckled. "Well, amazing for me, anyway. Drew's horse didn't want to go. He'd plant his hooves and yank the reins out of Drew's hands to eat grass, then realize the rest of the horses were vanishing up the trail and decide he needed to run and catch up. To hear Drew talk, you'd think the horse was doing some Kentucky Derby gallop through the woods, but he was barely trotting."

I laughed. "Oh, poor Drew! Is he okay? Will you ever be able to get him on a horse again?"

Bree rolled her eyes. "He's fine. He swears the only horses he's riding from now on are the ones outside of the Walmart that rock back and forth if you stick a quarter in the slot."

"How did Caleb and Courtney fare?" I asked.

"Good. I don't think they loved it as much as me, but they had fun. Courtney gets quiet sometimes. I don't blame her for being depressed and distracted. I probably shouldn't say anything, but Caleb mentioned to us that her brother passed away last month, and she's having a hard time coping."

Caleb had said the same to me, including that he'd hoped the vacation would help Courtney process her grief. "I'm so sorry to hear that. Was his death unexpected?"

Bree nodded. "I don't know the details. I mean, we just met them last week here at the campground, and I didn't want to pry, but from what Caleb said he was in his early-thirties, and it was a real shock. I think...I think from a few things Courtney mentioned that he may have committed suicide. But I shouldn't gossip, especially when I don't know all the facts."

"Oh, that's so tragic!" I exclaimed.

"She seems to be better this week," Bree added. "I think getting away helped. We're from the Roanoke area ourselves, and I hope we can keep in touch. Maybe go out for dinner once a month, or do some local hikes together. They're a really nice couple."

"They are," I agreed, thinking that Drew and Bree were equally nice.

Bree left with the coffees, and the morning rush continued. I gave out trail maps, talked up our evening's activities, and sold more coffee and snack-packs than usual. By ten, all of the kayaks and canoes were rented and most of our guests were off site enjoying nature. A few had stayed behind, happy to relax in their campers or tents, or sit on the sandy beach area of the lake and soak up the morning sun. Three kids had asked if they could play with Elvis and they were out front, tossing a ball for him and playing tug-of-war with one of his rope toys while I kept an eye on them all from the little café table by the window.

Mom came in and I excused Elvis from play, taking the hound for a nice long hike while on my break. There were still rhododendrons in bloom in the shady areas of the trail, and I took time to enjoy the dusky pink and white blooms. At the high point of the trail I sat at the rocky outcropping overlooking the lake and drank some water while Elvis sniffed around the trees and scrubby bushes. By the time we'd made it back to the campsite, I'd worked up a decent sweat and Elvis was panting. Things were quiet at the camp store, so we went back to the house where I could freshen up and change into less fragrant clothing.

My hamper was overflowing, and I realized that I'd need to do laundry in the next day or risk running out of clean clothes.

"There's no time like the present," I said to Elvis as I hauled the hamper across the room to the door. The hound eyed me, then dropped his head to the floor, eyes closing.

I left him sleeping and dragged the hamper to the laundromat, somehow managing to fit the contents into one washer. I'd just hit "start" on the machine when the door to the laundry room squeaked open, then closed with a *slap* sound. Turning around I saw Mickey walk in, a small basket of clothes under one arm. She still had some pink spots of Calamine on her arms and legs and I itched in sympathy.

"Ooo, the second washer is fixed!" she exclaimed. "I came in yesterday and we were down to one, so I only did a quick load. Now I don't feel so bad about doing the rest of my wash."

She moved over to the other washer and began to put her clothes in. I wondered if she'd been the one who'd left the clothes in the washer yesterday morning—the clothes another camper had set on the folding table. I didn't really want to ask and possibly alienate a multi-week guest, so I decided not to confront her about the clothes. She might have had a good reason for leaving them in the washer. Maybe she'd had a conference call that ran late or some other work emergency and couldn't get back here to put them in the dryer. Maybe she'd gotten busy and forgotten until afternoon. I'd post some rules, and just hope this had been a one-time mishap.

But just in case…

"I've been meaning to put a note up about the laundry facilities," I told her. "It's our busy season, and we've only got the two washers and two dryers for now—if I can keep them all running, that is. I didn't realize how much people used them, so I think it's a good idea to post a few basic rules. Things like making sure people get their clothes out of the machines right away, that they give the washer and the dryer a quick wipe after use, especially if their clothes are muddy. Things like that."

"Oh no. Did someone complain?" Mickey asked. "I saw my wash was on the table when I came back for it. I'm so sorry if another guest was inconvenienced. I try to set a timer on my phone if I have to leave when my clothes are in a machine, but I got caught up on a work call, then forgot all about them."

"It happens. I was going to throw them in the dryer for you, but I saw there was a stain on some of the clothes and didn't want it to set in."

"It was barbeque sauce," she hurriedly replied. "I was making a batch of it and the bowl spilled."

"Ugh. I hope you got it out," I said, taking out my phone

and setting the timer to remind me to take my clothes out of the washer.

Mickey didn't reply, so I wished her a good day and headed back to the house to plan dinner.

Friday would be a busy night with the bonfire and other activities, so I needed something fast, and something that would keep because we might need to be flexible about when we got away to eat dinner. Surveying the contents of the fridge, I put together a huge salad. Romaine with some spring greens for added flavor and some iceberg lettuce for added crunch. Tomatoes, broccoli rabe, and zucchini. Feeling inspired, I added diced salami, feta cheese, and chopped olives to make it a kitchen-sink mix of a salad. Then I made an oil and vinegar dressing with fresh basil, leaving that in its own bottle to add right before serving.

To soup or not to soup, that was the question. The salad seemed like it might be enough for dinner, but most days lunch wasn't exactly a hearty meal and breakfast tended to be whatever we could grab and eat as we worked, so I hated to have the salad as our only option.

Making a decision, I threw some ground beef in a skillet, browned it, then drained it before putting it in the Crock-Pot with minced onion, ketchup, brown sugar, mustard, Worcestershire sauce, a sprinkle of chili powder, and enough water to turn it into a sauce. I set the pot on low to cook until dinnertime. There. Sloppy Joe on some Kaiser rolls to go with our salad. And if it didn't get eaten, it would keep in the fridge to be warmed up for lunch tomorrow.

I'd just finished when the timer on my phone went off, so I jogged over to the laundromat to switch my clothes into the dryer before a guest needed to use the washer. I was shoulder-deep in the washer, rooting around for those stray socks that always seemed to live at the bottom of the wash pile, when I heard a familiar metallic rattle.

I was forever sticking change in my pockets and not checking when I did the laundry, but when I looked down into the washer drum, it wasn't quarters and nickels I saw, but a necklace.

A pretty gold chain with a gold heart pendant studded with diamond chips on one side. I examined it closely, noticing the missing ring on one side of the chain that would have been used to hook into the clasp. I'd checked the washer before putting my clothes in since sometimes there was a sock or, worse, a pair of underwear left behind by the previous user. The necklace hadn't been in there then, and besides that, I recognized it. I'd picked up this necklace outside of Danielle's barn when we'd taken her back to get her tools. Then I'd promptly forgotten about it after Elvis had found a dead body in her pot field.

Snapping a quick pic with my cell phone, I texted the image to Danielle, asking her if she'd lost a necklace.

It took her only a few seconds to respond in the negative. She'd never seen it before.

I frowned, then texted her back.

You don't remember anyone wearing it? Someone who visited you in the day or two before you drove in to rescue Squeakers?

I had found it right outside her barn. I remembered bending down to pick it up, and thinking that someone must have recently dropped it. Now it was squeaky clean after having gone through a wash and spin cycle, but when I'd found it, the necklace had been clean and in good condition. There weren't smashed or damaged links from someone driving over it. There wasn't dirt or debris on the necklace. It was on top of the gravel, not half buried under the rocks.

Someone had *just* dropped it, probably the day I'd found it, or at most a day or two earlier.

Danielle texted back, repeating that she'd never seen the

necklace before and that she hadn't had any visitors since the previous week.

I spread the necklace out on a paper towel and looked at it carefully, thinking that Danielle surely would have noticed it if someone had dropped it the day before or even the morning of the murder. It had been right there, in front of the barn in plain view.

The barn where the police had found the murder weapon. I caught my breath, realizing that there was a good chance the necklace had been dropped by the murderer.

And with that thought, my next text was to Jake.

CHAPTER 17

"Do you think the killer is a woman?" I asked Jake. "Or maybe the murderer was a man who dropped it out of his pocket?"

Although I didn't know why a man would be carrying around a loose necklace in his pocket. If he'd bought it as a gift, it would have been in a box or a bag. And the ring to the clasp was missing. I'd searched the washer, even pulling the filter and checking the drain hoses to see if maybe it had come off during the wash cycle, but hadn't found the ring. That led me to believe it had come off the wearer's neck in front of the barn, maybe caught on the tamping rod as they carried it and broken free.

Jake slid the necklace from the paper towel into a plastic evidence bag. "You think it was dropped that day?" he said, not answering my question.

I nodded. "Danielle says it's not hers, and where I found it...I can't believe she wouldn't have seen it. She'd said she was working on equipment in the barn that morning, and she'd pulled the tractor out to go rescue Squeakers. If it had been there before that, she would have driven right over it if she hadn't seen it herself and picked it up. And I *know* it wasn't driven over. I remember thinking it looked like someone had just dropped it recently, not that it had been there in the elements for a while, having people step on it or equipment crushing it into the gravel."

"We'll check it out," he told me. "If anyone reports a missing necklace and it ends up not being related to the crime scene, then we can return it to the rightful owner."

I snorted. "How the heck could it *not* be related to the crime scene? Someone dropped it between when Danielle left with her tractor to help Squeakers and when we got there. Whoever it belonged to was on Danielle's farm when the murder was committed, and they were right outside the barn where the murderer got the weapon and returned it. If the owner isn't the murderer, then they saw the whole thing. Which makes them an accessory, right? Was it a two-person job? Husband and wife? Boyfriend and girlfriend? Or did the woman with the necklace kill Wilber Kendricks?"

My mind raced through female suspects, and came up blank. This didn't look like the sort of necklace that the ex-wife, Marsha Kendricks would wear, and I couldn't think of any reason Wilber's daughter would come down from Chicago to kill her father at the edge of a marijuana field.

Plus, I had the nagging suspicion I'd seen this necklace before. Although it could just be my imagination or wishful thinking on my part. It didn't seem like a unique, original design. Lots of women wore necklaces with gold hearts on them, and I was sure many had small diamonds along one side as well. I could be just remembering a necklace I'd seen a co-worker wear last year, or one of the women at the meetings at the community center, or even at that CAD meeting Lottie and I went to.

I frowned, trying to remember if Gwen Sarlet had worn any jewelry, and came up blank.

"Is the murderer a woman?" I asked Jake again. "I talked to Marsha Kendricks and I can't believe she would have killed her ex-husband. Maybe it was someone Wilber was squeezing for money, someone who owned one of the businesses he was in charge of inspecting when he was in liquor compliance. Marsha said she suspected he was blackmailing people and taking payoffs when they were married."

Jake rolled his eyes. "We're working the case, Sassy. And yes, we're aware that there were complaints over the last few decades of Wilber Kendricks blackmailing businesses. The agency he worked for checked into the allegations and didn't find anything that supported the accusations of corruption. People get mad, and sometimes people think a write up by the inspector is biased or unfair. Sometimes they think they'll get back at the inspector by filing a complaint, but the agency said in the end, it was their word against Kendricks's."

"Did they send out a second investigator to see if the citations were legitimate?" I pressed, certain that Kendricks was dirty and that his illicit activities were related to his murder.

"It's easy for the establishment to fix the problem before a second investigator gets there," Jake countered. "So that's not necessarily proof that Kendricks was making up the citations to fuel a blackmail scheme."

"But even if Kendricks was totally clean, which I doubt, the people who complained might *think* he was doing them wrong," I argued. "They could be angry enough to want him dead, especially if the state liquor control board dismissed their complaints."

"We realize that, Sassy. We're checking all this out as well as some other leads. Trust that we'll find the killer, okay?"

I grumbled a little under my breath. "I've helped. Elvis and I found the inspector's car and that gas can."

"Yes, that was very helpful. And we got quite a few prints and other evidence off both," Jake replied.

"And I found the necklace," I continued. "Civilians can be useful in investigations. Sometimes a civilian who saw something or heard something, or happened to have a security camera with footage helps solve a case."

"That's true. I'm not discounting your help here." Jake sighed. "If I tell you a few things, will you promise to stay out of this investigation? I appreciate you calling me when you find something out, but I'd prefer you stay here and safely run your campground. Whoever murdered Wilber Kendricks might not think twice about killing a nosy woman snooping around in the case."

I thought of Mom's panic over a possible Mafia involvement and decided Jake had a point. I couldn't guarantee I wouldn't be nosy or continue to snoop around, but I'd maybe wait a day or two before diving back into my amateur sleuth hobby.

Except we were supposed to go to the Twelve Gauge tomorrow, and I'd planned on asking some questions of the owner or manager. Maybe that didn't count as snooping or interfering in the investigation? I could just be curious about alcohol inspections. It was important to expand my knowledge, and it was good to want to learn about a broad range of topics.

Because everyone had to have a hobby. Mom had knitting and bridge, and evidently white-hat hacking. My new hobby seemed to be solving crimes. And it wasn't my fault that Reckless seemed to have more than its fair share of crime.

"Okay. I'll stay out of the case, but if you all haven't solved it by tomorrow noon, I'm not going to be held responsible for any snooping I do," I told Jake.

He laughed. "Fair enough. So here's some information to keep up my end of the bargain. We're looking into those complaints about Wilber Kendricks blackmailing people."

I sniffed. "You already told me that, so it doesn't really

count as new information. Did you find the money? If he was truly blackmailing people, I doubt Kendricks would have kept two decades worth of illicit gains in his sock drawer. There had to be some questionable deposits in his bank accounts that you can flag."

"We've got a forensic accountant working that," Jake explained. "And we've got a list of business owners who complained as well as those that were fined and those that went under in the last two years. It's a big list. Lots of bars and restaurants don't make it their first five years. It's a tough business, and there are a lot of places that just go under due to financial issues. Still, we're looking into each of them."

I nodded, thinking that's exactly what I would do if I were more than a snoop. "Are any of those businesses owned by women?" I asked, thinking of the necklace.

"A few. But we're not ruling out those owned by men right now either. It could be a wife or a daughter who thinks Kendricks is to blame for their misfortune." Jake glanced around then leaned in closer to me. "There were several calls to the Cannabis Control Authority in the week before Kendricks was murdered, asking about his schedule. The first call, a woman said she was a reporter doing an article on the program and was hoping to meet up with him at a farm for an interview and photo op. The person who took the call refused to give the information out and instead took a message. The number that the caller gave went to a grocery store in Richmond, and the name given didn't check out with any reporters at the paper she supposedly worked for. The next call was a woman claiming to be Wilber's daughter, who asked again for his schedule. This time the person who took the call gave the information out, thinking it would be nice for the man's daughter to surprise him and take him to lunch."

I sucked in a breath. "So it *was* a woman."

"Or a woman and a man together," he reminded me. "We're pulling phone records to see what number the incoming calls came from, and I'm hoping to have that information in the next day at most."

"So, you should get that information before I come off my snooping hiatus and get my nose back into the case?" I teased him. "If I had known there was a chance you'd solve this in the next twenty-four hours, I wouldn't have promised to stay out of it."

"I feel better with you on the sidelines, but I'm pretty sure your snooping would have reached a dead end," Jake told me. "If it's someone who Wilber Kendricks had blackmailed, then it's probably not a local. Before he moved to cannabis inspections, all of his clients were in Roanoke County. He didn't handle any bars or dining establishments in this area."

That meant the killer would have driven here to murder the inspector, then promptly driven home. Jake was right, the chances I'd find the killer or any further evidence, were slim to none.

"Still, you do seem to be a magnet for this kind of crime," Jake added. "So promise me you'll stay out of it? Please?"

How could I say no when he asked so nicely? But I knew my nature, and just like Elvis, if a clue came within range of my nose, I was compelled to follow it.

"I'll be careful," I said. "I'll try not to go confronting any possible murder suspects. And if I find anything out, I'll call you or Deputy Sean. Is that good enough?"

It would have to be because I'd promised Mom we could go to the Twelve Gauge tomorrow at lunch, and I wasn't about to pass up the opportunity to at least do a little research.

And speaking of research, my mother had some skills that I'd never realized. I planned on taking advantage of those skills and satisfying my curiosity. But not tonight. Tonight I had a bonfire and several campground activities to run.

Tomorrow I'd satisfy my curiosity. And at noon, my snooping would be back in action.

Jake eyed the easels and paint kits set up along the dock as I walked him to his truck. "Is that your thing tonight? Watercolors by the lake?"

"With wine," I informed him. "I don't think I could get many people to paint scenic landscapes without wine."

He laughed. "There isn't enough wine in the world to get me to paint a scenic landscape. The end result would probably wind up in the burn pile. I don't have an artistic bone in my body."

"The joy is in the doing, not necessarily in the finished product," I said. "A beautiful sunset view, lively conversation, a fun and probably humorous attempt at art, and wine. What's not to like?"

"Uh, the art? The rest sounds like a perfect evening. Why ruin it all by adding art into the mix?"

I rolled my eyes. "Well, thirty of my guests think otherwise, thankfully."

"Are the kids painting as well?" he asked. "Do you have fruit juice in sippy cups for them instead of wine?"

"The children are welcome to join in with a non-alcoholic beverage, but most of them are more interested in the balloon sculpture activity."

A few of the adults were likewise interested in the balloon sculpture class, which had surprised me. I guess twisting balloons into dogs and hats was considered ageless fun.

"I'm assuming that's the balloon sculpture instructor and not the sip-and-paint instructor," Jake said, pointing to a man climbing out of a blue compact car.

The man was wearing a clown outfit, complete with a frizzy orange wig and facial makeup.

CHAPTER 18

"Oh no." When I'd spoken with Simon Marconi and arranged for the class, he'd not been attired as a clown. I'd assumed he'd show up at the campsite looking much like he had the day I'd met him and not like someone performing in a circus show.

"I take it you're one of those people who's afraid of clowns?" Jake's eyes danced with amusement.

"I don't have any problem with clowns, but I'm worried some of my guests will. It's not a good thing to have campers freaked out and spending their second night on vacation tossing and turning with clown nightmares."

Jake grinned as he opened the door to his truck. "May I suggest more wine?"

More wine wasn't going to avoid clown-fueled nightmares, so I left Jake starting up his truck and made my way over to the orange-haired man pulling a box of supplies out of the backseat of his car.

"Um, Simon?" I said as I approached. "I didn't expect you to run the class dressed as a clown."

He turned around and grabbed his red ball of a nose. It made a honking sound, like that of a bicycle horn. "Happy Honkers is a hit at every kid's party. And this is a kids' party, right?"

"Kind of. I mean, it's mostly kids but some adults as well. I just didn't...when I met with you, you weren't dressed as Happy Honkers. And the picture in the paper from the party at the senior center didn't have you dressed as Happy Honkers either."

"The senior center specifically requested Happy not be present," he explained. "It seems some of the residents aren't fans. But this is how I do all the other gigs. Is it a problem? Do you not like Happy?"

I was ambivalent about Happy, and it was honestly too late for me to ask him to change and remove all that makeup at this point. Plus, I didn't want to hurt the guy's feelings. Confrontation wasn't the easiest thing for me, and the man seemed a whole lot more vulnerable with a clown face and orange hair than he had while I was chatting with him at the Community Center a few weeks ago.

I'd have to just go with it, and hope none of my guests had clown phobias.

I led Happy/Simon to the firepit where Austin was getting ready to light the giant stack of wood. He glanced up, his eyes widening when he saw the clown. I ignored him, showing Happy where to put his supplies and getting him a bottle of water to drink.

A few children were already starting to gather near the firepit area, and Happy Honkers was definitely getting their attention. They approached the clown, asking him questions about what he was doing and Simon slipped right into his act, honking his nose-horn and handing out balloons for the children to begin blowing up, instructing them on exactly how much air to fill the balloons with to facilitate making their sculptures. He blew up balloons for the younger ones, and soon a dozen children were fighting with balloon swords while the clown engaged them in sword play.

Within ten minutes, there were as many adults doing the same, joking and whacking each other with balloon swords, replenishing their weapons when they popped or deflated.

Austin got the fire going, and my relief over no one being panicked by the clown in our midst faded as I realized balloons and fire didn't exactly mix.

Thankfully any upset children were quickly placated by the endless supply of replacement balloons that Happy had available.

As dinnertime came and went, more campers arrived at the bonfire. Several sat in their folding chairs, drinking beer and chatting with newfound friends. Others joined the fun with the children and the clown. The participants moved from making balloon swords to balloon dogs, to balloon hats, a few of the adults straying into more naughty balloon sculptures as the sun dipped over the lake.

The phallic balloon sculptures *were* funny, but they weren't exactly the tone I wanted to set for my family-friendly campground. Thankfully none of the kids seemed to notice the unusual designs, and before things got too lurid, it was time to shift the adults over to the paint-and-sip activity by the docks.

"You've got the kids?" I asked Mom as the instructor for the painting activity clapped her hands and instructed the participants to follow her.

"Austin and I will make sure everyone here is safe and enjoying themselves," Mom informed me. "Including the clown. I'll admit I had my doubts when I saw him arrive. I mean, I knew you'd hired a balloon artist, I just didn't expect him to arrive with a red nose that honks and an orange afro. You didn't mention that he was a clown."

"I didn't know he was a clown," I admitted, thinking that I probably needed to do a little more research on the people I was hiring for campground activities.

"Well, either way, the guy is a hit. With both the children and the adults." Mom gestured over to where Caleb, Courtney, Drew, and Bree were busy twisting their balloons into the shape of dogs.

"You know Courtney's brother died recently?" I said to Mom. "Bree thinks it might have been a suicide. Caleb said he was hoping this vacation would help her begin to move on from her grief."

Mom nodded. "I talked to her the day after they checked in and she told me about her brother. So tragic. She was doubting whether the vacation was a good idea, and said she was really struggling to get through each day. She said that she didn't get out of bed for two days after he'd died. She barely made it through his funeral without breaking down. I told her how hard it had been when your father passed away. When someone is such a big part of your life, it's difficult to imagine going on without them."

"Mom. I'm so sorry." I'd known she'd grieved when Dad died, but honestly I'd been wrapped up in my own sorrow and hadn't truly realized the pain my mother must have been feeling under her capable exterior.

"I'd told her that it had helped me to find purpose in each day. In the beginning, I'd wake up each morning and dedicated my day to Owen. In time, I was able to shift my focus back to myself and what I wanted my life to be—which is what your father would have wanted. But in the beginning, making each day a memorial helped me to continue on without him."

I glanced again over at Courtney, thinking that my

mother's words and the vacation must have helped. She did seem different from when she'd arrived, not that I'd realized she was grieving then. At the time, I'd just thought her quiet, solemn, and maybe not as into camping as her husband. Her disappearing every day into town to explore and do some shopping reinforced my original opinion. But the shopping must have helped as well. Maybe the alone time in the stores and antique shops gave her time to process the loss of her brother. Maybe her and Caleb's budding friendship with Drew and Bree helped heal the wounds. Either way, she seemed a different person from the woman who'd checked in a week ago. There were still times when her gaze fixed on a point somewhere in the distance, and her thoughts probably turned sorrowful, but I frequently saw her as she was now, laughing and joking, and clearly enjoying the moment.

Mom went over to join the kids in their latest balloon sculpture with Happy Honkers. Austin tended the bonfire. I checked my list of paint-and-sip enrollees and walked around the area to corral any stragglers. I'd set up some extra stations, thinking that I might have a few last-minute sign-ups. A bonfire, balloon swords, and a beer or two might convince a few more guests that a sunset paint-and-sip was an ideal way to end their evening.

Mickey was on my list, so I made my way around the bonfire to where she was sitting alone, a red balloon hat on her head, and a yellow balloon sword on her lap. I felt a twinge of sadness that she was by herself when so many of the other campers were socializing with their friends, family, or other guests. Maybe she was just a loner. She'd certainly had not seemed shy the times I'd talked with her over the last week, but that didn't mean she was an outgoing person. Plus, I figured it must be hard, being surrounded by new people each week in the campground and moving her home-on-wheels every month. It seemed like that would make it hard to form lasting friendships.

"Are you still up for the paint-and-sip?" I asked with a smile.

"Oh, gosh!" She got up, balloon sword in hand. "Sorry, I'd forgotten that was tonight. It's been a crazy few days with work, and I've lost track of what time, or even day, it is."

"They're just getting ready," I assured her. "You're not late, but you should probably head over now."

"Here." She handed me her sword so she could collapse her chair and tuck it under her arm. "Can you give it to one of the kids, or just toss it? I don't think I can manage carrying my chair, a sword, and a finished painting."

"No problem." I brandished the sword with a smile, thinking I'd let Mom or Austin have it to battle the kids.

Mickey walked toward the dock and I moved around the campfire, urging people I knew had signed up to head over to the paint-and-sip activity. Seeing Bree, I went toward the four adults, and asked her if she was still interested in the paint-and-sip activity.

"Yes! Sorry, I seem to have gotten a little over-enthusiastic about my balloon hat and lost track of time." Bree turned to Courtney. "Are you signed up to do the paint-and-sip?"

"I didn't…" Courtney's voice trailed off and she looked at me with an expectant expression.

"There's room available, but hurry up before the instructor gets started," I told the two women. "There's wine and plastic cups on the table next to the dock, so get a drink and get painting."

The girls headed toward the dock, squealing and poking each other with their balloon swords.

Caleb smiled, eyeing his wife fondly. "She really enjoyed

the balloon activity. Actually, she's really enjoyed everything the last few days. We're planning on doing some more hiking tomorrow morning if her poison ivy isn't too bad. And maybe we'll go visit that bird sanctuary after lunch. I'm trying to find interesting activities to keep her out of the stores or at least doing something with me instead of by herself. What do *you* usually do around here on your days off?"

I laughed. "That would be *day* off, as in singular. Actually I haven't even had a full day without work since I bought the campground, but I try to grab a few hours here and there to hike. When I'm off for a few hours, I like to go into town and relax with Elvis at the coffee shop, or sit on the dock with a book. Tuesday I witnessed the rescue of a pig off a porch roof."

And found a dead body, but I wasn't about to tell him that.

"A *pig*? On a *porch*? In Reckless?" Caleb grinned. "I'd pay good money to see that."

"Well if you'd like to see the famous pig, Squeakers, he often hangs out at the Bait and Beer. He likes to watch the guys play board games. Checkers is his favorite, I'm told."

Caleb shook his head. "Does the pig play? I've heard they're really smart."

"I've never seen him play, but who knows? There are stranger things in the world than a pig playing checkers."

"True." He stood and brushed off his pants, then dug two beers out of the ice chest before turning to Drew. "You want to go watch the girls paint? Or stay here and make balloon hats?"

Drew tossed his balloon sword aside and stood. "Can we paint too? I'm normally not the artsy-fartsy type, but I've had a few beers and the idea of painting and drinking kinda appeals to me right now."

Eat your heart out, Jake. See? Booze did increase the desire to do artistic endeavors.

"There's room," I said, adding their names onto my reserve list. "You can drink your own beers, or get a plastic cup of wine on the table by the dock. But hurry. They've probably already started painting the backgrounds."

CHAPTER 19

*I*t seemed especially dark on my pre-dawn walk with Elvis the next morning. With some concern, I searched the skies and found no stars. Not even a blurry hint of a moon filtered through the thick clouds overhead. Once we were back to the camp store and I had poured myself a cup of coffee, I pulled up the forecast and grimaced.

A drought wouldn't be good for anyone in the county, and I knew the small showers we'd had here and there over the last few months weren't enough for the farmers, the foliage, or the lake, but campgrounds weren't much fun on rainy days.

The weather app said to expect a cloudy day with rain in the afternoon. That was a bit of a bummer as far as hiking and lake activities went, but the occasional rainy day was to be expected when running a campground. It wasn't the afternoon showers that caused my frown though, it was the line of thunderstorms marching in a menacing fashion across the Doppler radar map.

Storms worried me. I hoped the repairs on the one cabin

roof held, and that the others didn't suffer any leaks. I hoped my guests with RVs and campers had taken them in to be caulked and sealed recently. I hoped my tent campers had taken care in choosing their setup area, and had their rain-flies ready to go. My guests would probably want to spend this evening inside since it looked like the storms would hit late afternoon and last well into the night. I'd need to make sure we were fully stocked at the camp store, and that the game room was clean and organized for anyone who wanted to spend a rainy night playing ping-pong or board games.

The game room was mostly open space with a few tables, two arcade machines, and a ping-pong table. The closet held all sorts of board games, but I'd never checked them to ensure they had all of the pieces. Likewise with the ping-pong equipment. I knew the arcade machines worked, but with the weather being so nice, few of my guests had ever bothered venturing to the game room. Today might mark a shift in that trend.

I made a quick note for Austin to go through the games and locate the ping-pong equipment, and to also ensure the tables and chairs were in safe condition.

My phone beeped, and I read the warning scrolling across the screen in yellow. Severe thunderstorm watch from three o'clock to nine o'clock. We should expect torrential rain, strong winds, and conditions for flash flooding.

Great. Just great.

I'd never been in a campground during a major storm and wasn't sure what to expect. Would the cabins hold up in high winds, or leak? Would guest's RVs and campers do the same? Those poor tent people were going to be in big trouble in strong winds, let alone torrential rains and flash floods. I'd need to make sure we had enough space in the game room to house any tent campers who might find their equipment not up to withstanding the weather.

Pulling out the roster, I glanced at the number of guests on the tent sites, did some quick math and realized that we couldn't comfortably fit thirty people in the game room—not if they all needed to sleep on the floor, anyway. If the storm wasn't too bad, we might only get ten or fifteen people needing to use the space overnight, but I needed to think about what I'd do during a truly violent storm. Even if this one wasn't as bad as the weather app predicted, eventually we'd get terrible weather, and I'd never really planned for how I'd manage to shelter eighty or more guests.

Storms. Tornados. Hail. Wind gusts. My mind raced through all the possible disasters. And if we had a drought, and there was a fire in the forest...

I took a deep breath and tried to steer my brain away from worst-case scenario thinking. For tonight, we had the game room for those who needed shelter. And we could use the camp store for overflow. And our house, if needed. If things got really bad, there was also the laundromat and the shower rooms. They'd be horribly uncomfortable, but sleeping there would be better than being cold, wet, and possibly blown halfway across the forest.

Just as I tacked the note for Austin up on the register, Sierra's van pulled into the lot. Flora got out and grabbed the first box of food orders out of the back of the van. As she came into the store, a few guests followed. The dreary gray morning skies didn't seem to put off the intrepid campers, and I was soon busy with food orders, purchases, and inquiries about possible activities for the day—rain or shine.

By the time Mom got in at ten, all the kayaks and canoes had been rented, and I was busy straightening shelves and stocking the activity fliers that had been snatched up like they were half-off coupons at an electronics store. I briefed Mom on the morning's activities, warning her about the day's potentially rainy weather and the severe storm watch for tonight.

Mom bit her lip in thought. "Maybe we shouldn't go to the Twelve Gauge for lunch after all. I mean, if it's going to rain, then we're going to have a whole lot of campers to entertain this afternoon. And a storm…. I'd hate to leave Austin to handle things on his own, especially if guests need shelter during the storm."

"It shouldn't start raining until we get back," I pointed out. "And Lottie agreed to come help Austin out, so he won't need to handle things on his own."

Mom had been so looking forward to this outing that I hated to postpone it. And the storm wasn't predicted to arrive until late afternoon or early evening. We should be back hours before that. And honestly if it started raining early, Lottie and Austin should be able to direct any bored campers to the game room.

"I really want to go this afternoon," I added. "We need a break, and it will be fun to do something together."

Even if doing something together meant going to a dive bar with a questionable reputation and probably equally questionable food choices.

"Are you sure?" Mom asked. "We can always go next week. I hate for us to saddle Austin and poor Lottie with a campground full of bored guests to entertain."

"A good number of people went into town to explore the shops, and visit the Savage Lake Historical Exhibit at the Community Center. Others are trying to get their hiking and fishing in early, saying they'll just relax in their cabins or campers if the rain starts. And there's the game room for any campers who don't want to curl up and read inside their tents. They'll all be fine. Besides, we'll be back by two at the latest."

"Okay." Mom sounded hesitant. "If you're sure."

It was funny how me, the workaholic, was the one urging us to go, while Mom was wanting to postpone our trip. But I was trying to change. And a little rain wasn't going to keep us from having fun.

"I'm sure," I told her.

CHAPTER 20

$\mathcal{T}$he Twelve Gauge was a short one-story building that looked like it might have at one time been a convenience store and gas station. The pumps were gone, but the overhang remained, shielding a handful of weathered picnic tables from the sun and rain.

We pulled into the parking lot and I noted that, in addition to my SUV, there were three motorcycles, an old diesel Mercedes sedan, and a pickup truck with literal duct table holding the front fender together parked there. The motorcycles were the nicest vehicles in the lot, including mine. They were all shiny chrome, tall handlebars, and silver-studded leather saddle pads. Mom and I got out, and I hit the button to lock the SUV more out of habit than the need to safeguard any contents or the vehicle. Walking in the door, we paused for a second, blinking to let our eyes adjust to the dim light.

A few dozen unoccupied high-top tables lay between us and the long straight bar. Three men that I took to be the owners of the motorcycles from their attire were at the far end of the bar, sipping beer and devouring burgers and fries as they conversed. A man in grease-stained coveralls who was staring with rapt attention at the television behind the bar sat three stools down, a soda and a plate of nachos in front of him. The other patron was a woman who looked to be about Mom's age with her silver hair bundled into a complicated up-do. She wore a pair of pink hot-pants and a screaming yellow tank top, and had an entire cosmetics counter worth of makeup on, including a thick application of sky-blue eyeshadow.

Of course, Mom made a beeline for the bikers.

"Is this seat taken?" she asked one, plopping herself down right next to him before he could even reply.

Which left me to take the seat next to her, putting only one seat between me and television-watching-man.

"Ooo, that burger looks good," Mom said, leaning over to inspect the food of the man next to her. "Do you boys eat here often? What do you recommend?"

I grimaced, twisting so I could catch the man's eye. "I'm so sorry. Mom, these men are having lunch together. We're disturbing them. We should go sit farther down the bar, or at one of the tables."

"If we're bothering you, we can move," Mom told him, her gaze drifting down the bar toward the woman with the colorful attire.

"Not at all," the man next to her said. "We're out for our Saturday ride, although we'll probably have to head home right after lunch to try and beat the rain."

"Us too," Mom said. "Actually, we're not too worried about the rain, but we do want to beat those storms coming in tonight. If I were on a bike, I'd want to get back too. I never felt safe being on a motorcycle in the rain."

I blinked, wondering when Mom was on a motorcycle. I filed that away, figuring that might be a good topic of conversation for later.

"I'm Ellie Mae Letouroux," Mom announced, sticking out her hand. "And this is my daughter, Sassy."

"Duncan," the man next to her said, shaking her hand. "And this is Kevin and Stu."

"Nice to meet you all," I said as the men nodded their hellos.

Thankfully the bartender appeared from the back before this became even *more* awkward than it already was.

The bartender was a twenty-something woman with bright red hair, a nose ring, and dark, precise, geometrically shaped eyebrows. She handed us a couple of menus, put two bundles of silverware rolled in napkins in front of us, then asked what we wanted to drink.

"What wines do you have?" Mom asked.

"Red, white, pink, and fizzy," the bartender announced.

Mom pursed her lips in thought. "What's that lady at the end of the bar drinking?"

"Jim Beam and seltzer," the bartender replied.

Yikes. I'd be passed out on the bar before my lunch arrived.

"What's on tap?" I asked, craning my neck to see if I recognized any of the tap handles. With our wine selection being red, white, pink, or fizzy, I didn't hold out much hope for a decent beer.

To my surprise, along with the usual domestic beers, the Twelve Gauge had several craft beers on tap as well as Guinness Stout. Clearly this was a beer bar, and not so much of a wine bar.

"I'll take a Guinness," I told the bartender.

"I want Jim Beam with a splash of seltzer," Mom announced.

My eyes shot wide. "Seriously? You haven't had hard liquor in years—not since that margarita at Colton's wedding. I didn't think you even liked whisky."

"Maybe I'll like it with a splash of seltzer." Mom nodded toward the other woman at the end of the bar. "She seems to like it. At least, I suppose she does since she ordered it. I haven't seen her actually take a drink of the stuff so maybe it's not good."

The bartender let out a gigantic sigh. "Do you want me to come back later? Give you a little more time to decide?"

"No, I've changed my mind. I think I'll have a Guinness as well," Mom said. "You're right. Jim Beam and seltzer probably isn't a good choice, especially since I'll need to work when we get back and won't have time to sleep off a drunk."

"Good decision," Duncan informed her. "The burgers are excellent here. And the jalapeño poppers as well."

"And the Rosetta chicken," Stu added. "I like it with mashed potatoes and peas."

Rosetta chicken? I glanced over the menu, seriously intrigued, but found no listing for Rosetta chicken. Was it a special? Or maybe Stu had meant the Rotisserie Chicken instead. I was tempted to order it, but that bartender looked like she wasn't thrilled with Mom and me, and I didn't want to embarrass myself by calling it by the wrong name. Or worse, get something and not like it.

We ordered burgers and decided to split some jalapeño poppers. When our food came, we continued chatting with the three men, drank our beers, and ate. As soon as she was finished, Mom challenged the men to a game of darts. While they headed over to the board, I hailed down the bartender, wanting to see if the owner or manager was in.

"Is the owner in?" I asked as the woman approached, wiping her hands on a towel. "Or the manager?"

She narrowed her eyes. "Who's asking?"

"Sassy Letouroux," I replied. "They don't know me— either the owner or the manager. I just wanted to ask one of them some questions about running a bar—things like licensing, and inspections."

She stared at me a few seconds then walked away. I saw her head into the back, and wasn't sure if she was going to get the manager, or had decided to ignore my request. About ten minutes later a middle-aged man with a beard, a neck tattoo, and a belly that hung over the waistband of his pants walked out of the back room and over to me.

"I'm the owner, Dean." He put out his hand. "Are you planning on opening up some competition? Or maybe one of those fancy whisky bars like they've got in Roanoke?"

"Oh no, not at all." I shook his hand. "I'm Sassy Letouroux. I bought the Reckless Camper Campground this spring and I just wanted to ask a few questions," I added, hoping that my being another local business owner might make him a little more friendly.

"The campground? You're planning on putting a bar in at the campground? Is that why you want to know about licensing?" He shook his head in confusion. "Not sure if they'll approve that or not. You're probably better off getting that information online, or just calling the licensing board. I don't think I'd be of much help."

I glanced over at Mom as she threw a dart. It missed the board entirely, landing instead in the drywall. Judging from the amount of holes in the wall, she wasn't the only one who was truly terrible at darts, so I didn't feel the need to intervene or apologize.

"No, I don't want to open a bar," I said, turning back to Dean.

His eyebrows went up and he stared at me, waiting for me to explain. I felt my palms sweat a bit, and wiped them on my pants leg. This was ridiculous. I ran a business. I'd spent most of my working life handling trade shows and marketing for a large corporation. I might not like confrontation, but I was confident and assertive. Yet here I was, completely out of my element in a bar with a grumpy bartender and an owner who clearly had better things to do than talk to me on a Saturday afternoon.

"I just wanted to ask some questions because of the murder. See, I was out at Danielle Pouliette's farm and found the body of that cannabis inspector. Lottie Sinclair was giving her a ride home after her tractor had broken down trying to rescue Squeakers off Celeste Crenshaw's porch roof, and Elvis and I were tagging along," I babbled nervously. "The inspector's ex-wife said he used to be a health inspector, then an alcohol inspector before he became a cannabis inspector, and that she thought he might have been taking kickbacks or blackmailing people, and I wondered what sort of things an alcohol inspector might threaten a bar owner with that would get him or her shut down, because maybe there are a whole lot of people with motives to kill this guy besides Danielle and Scat."

Dean blinked, still confused. "Huh? I didn't get any of that. Well, I didn't get any of that except you having Elvis in someone's car. Was that an Elvis impersonator? His ghost? His preserved body?"

"My bloodhound. His name is Elvis." I took a deep breath and let it out, trying to calm down and not have this man think I was a complete fool. "Basically, a cannabis inspector was murdered, but he used to be an alcohol inspector in Roanoke, and I was just wondering what sort of things an alcohol inspector could accuse someone of—things that might get a business shut down if he wrote them up."

He motioned for me to sit at a high-top table, then took a seat across from me when I scooted myself into the chair. "Well, the biggie is serving to a minor. They'll send someone in to buy to see if you card them or not. Then there's watering down the liquor. They'll test a few bottles, to make sure you're not ripping customers off. They also look at your records to make sure you're buying liquor through the state and not selling booze you brought in from somewhere or from a non-licensed supplier. Then there's some cleanliness stuff about your glassware and your bar area. They want to make sure your garnishes are fresh and kept refrigerated. There's a certification bartenders and bar managers need to go through as well, and they'll check those. Pretty much anything a health inspector can nail you on, an alcohol inspector can as well." Dean shook his head. "Pain in the butt, but whatever. You gotta do what you gotta do."

I nodded. "If an inspector wanted to break the law and accuse a bar of something, then request a payoff to keep his mouth shut, what violation do you think he'd use?"

"Oh, definitely selling alcohol to minors, but any of the health ones or watering booze would work as well." Dean frowned. "Hey. You're not talking about Wilber Kendricks here, are you?"

I nodded, thinking there couldn't have been more than one cannabis inspector who'd been murdered in the past week. "Yes. Did you read about it in the paper? It's just a rumor. I don't have any proof that he was blackmailing people, but years ago someone close to him thought he might be, and there were some complaints to the state about his citations."

Dean snorted and shook his head. "It's no rumor. I've got a friend who owns a bar in Roanoke that he tried that stuff on. Kendricks quickly realized he was picking on the wrong business owner. Bulldog told him if he lied about his bar having violations, that Kendricks would end up in a fifty-gallon drum of lye buried in a field somewhere. Let's just say, Kendricks left and there were no citations on Bulldog's business. Next month, another inspector showed up—one who was on the right side of the law."

I couldn't help but stare at the man, my mouth wide open. Dean knew someone who'd been blackmailed—unsuccessfully, but still it was an attempted blackmail. So Wilber Kendricks *was* dirty. And there were probably a whole lot of restaurant and bar owners who'd paid him and might want him dead, as well as those who didn't pay and got a wrongful citation as a result. I was right, and Jake was on the right path by looking through not only the complaints against Kendricks, but the businesses he'd handled.

Not just the businesses that had gone under, though. Jake might need to look at *all* the businesses, because someone who was still open might have just gotten fed up with paying Kendricks and decided to kill him instead. They were all suspects.

Maybe even Dean's friend, Bulldog. Not that I was about to go confront someone named Bulldog, or anyone else for that matter.

Mom and the guys had finished playing their game of darts, and I was pretty sure my mother hadn't won that game. The bikers were leaving, trying to make it home before the rain, and Mom was heading over to the woman in the colorful clothing who was drinking Jim Beam and seltzer at the other end of the bar. I smiled, glad she was having a good time.

"One more thing," I asked Dean. "Do you have something on the menu called Rosetta chicken?"

CHAPTER 21

It turned out that there was a Rosetta chicken on special. Evidently it had a sliced tomato on it and some melted mozzarella cheese, and while I was glad I'd gotten the burger, I might give it a try next time.

Mom had a nice chat with the woman at the end of the bar, and now had plans to meet Rosalind for lunch next week. I was glad she was making friends, but the rain had moved in earlier than the weather app had predicted and fat drops had begun to splat against the windshield as we drove back to the campground.

I really didn't like the look of those dark clouds to the southwest of us. Hopefully Duncan, Kevin, and Stu had managed to get home and weren't still out riding their motorcycles in this.

"Are we going to beat the storm?" Mom asked, eyeing those same dark clouds.

"I hope so." The fat drops abruptly turned into a downpour and I slowed down as visibility lessened. Traffic was light, but I didn't want to accidentally overshoot a curve on this road and wind up in a ditch, or swerve into the other lane, unable to see the center lines with all the rain coming down.

"I wonder how Austin and Lottie are faring," Mom fretted as she took out her cell phone.

We weren't going to get back any faster even if there was an urgent situation at the campground, but Mom texted anyway.

"Lottie says they're fine. About twenty of the tent campers are holed up in the game room to wait out the rain. They're currently playing ping-pong, Scrabble, and Uno. She and Austin brought in a few coolers of drinks and some snacks to sell, and everyone seems in good spirits. The cabin and camper guests seem to be locked up tight in their quarters, so there's enough space right now in the game room."

"Maybe the tent campers should bring their sleeping bags and belongings into the game room, just in case their tents flood," I suggested, worried that I might have twenty to thirty people sleeping on a hard floor with only my spare towels and sheets for bedding.

Mom typed again on her phone, then told me the response. "After we left Austin went around to the tent campers and warned them there might be heavy rains and a storm coming in late this afternoon or tonight. He told them we'd have shelter in the game room, and to make sure their belongings were consolidated so they could grab-and-go if needed, and that their sleeping bags were packed up and off the ground. They spread the word to other campers who were out. Ooo, and Mickey just arrived with a huge pot of soup she cooked up in her camper. Isn't that nice? She got inside just before the downpour started."

I blew out a breath, relieved that if the storm turned bad, a third of my guests wouldn't be dealing with sodden bedding and clothing. They were snug and dry, and thanks to Mickey they had some hot food in addition to the snacks and drinks from the camp store as well as whatever they'd brought from their tents. I'd need to thank Mickey for her help. Actually, I needed to thank a lot of people.

Austin deserved a raise. And Lottie deserved a lot more than just dinner. They'd both shown me that I didn't have to carry the responsibility for the campground solely on my shoulders. Mom, Austin, Lottie, and even the other campers were there to help. It felt good to know that I had friends, and that people cared.

It took us nearly twenty minutes longer to get back from the Twelve Gauge than it took to get there, but we arrived in one piece. The rain hadn't let up at all, and the campground drive was rutted with flowing water that hadn't found a better route to drain. I tensed, thinking of flash floods and the damage they might cause not just to my property, but to all the others who had homes and farms in the area. It would take a lot for the lake to over overflow its banks, but there were so many streams and rivers in the area that *would* overflow if the rain kept up like this.

I slowed as we approached the house, not sure if I should take Mom there, or with me to the game room.

"Drop me at the house," Mom instructed. "I'm going to check for leaks. Then I'll gather up spare blankets and towels and cook up more soup in case we need it."

"Good idea." I eased into the parking area and up on the grass to get as close to the porch steps as possible. "I'll check on things at the game room, then go over to the camp store for any supplies we might need. It's probably a good idea to get candles and flashlights together just in case the storm knocks the power out."

"There's that pack of glow-sticks we found in the attic," Mom said. "We could go ahead and give them out to the kids, so if the electricity cuts, parents will be able to quickly locate them."

Another good idea.

I waited for Mom to get inside the house, then drove over to the game room. The rain was still coming down hard with no sign of letting up, so I made a mad dash for the door. I was completely soaked in the ten steps it took me to get from the SUV to the entrance.

"Miss Sassy! You're wet," Austin informed me as I stood on the entrance mat, dripping water.

Lottie handed me a towel and I wiped my face and hair, surveying the scene. There was no emergency. Everyone was relaxed and calm. Some sat on their sleeping bags or camp chairs reading or talking. A handful of campers had gotten into the board games, creatively using pennies and scraps of paper for missing pieces. Four people had what looked to be an incredibly competitive ping-pong game going on.

There was no need for Mom to bring by towels, because there were a whole stack of them beside the door. Flashlights and glowsticks too. Mickey had plugged in her CrockPot of soup in a corner and someone had found disposable bowls and plastic spoons as well.

I pulled my phone out of my pocket, wiped it dry with the towel, then quickly texted Mom, telling her to stay put. Lottie and Austin had everything handled. I'd stay here until the storm was over, then get everyone situated for the night before returning home.

"Where's Elvis?" I asked, suddenly realizing I hadn't seen the hound.

"Over there." Austin pointed to the far side of the room where Elvis had sprawled out on the ground. Three little girls were fawning over him, feeding him Cheez-It crackers. No wonder he hadn't come over to greet me. Food ranked high on Elvis's priority list.

Lightning lit up the storm-darkened sky outside and a peal of thunder shook the building. The lights flickered, but thankfully stayed on. A few children squealed, but the adults laughed and kept on with their games. It warmed my heart that they felt safe here, that the campground had been able to provide them with shelter during the storm.

I made the rounds, talking with the guests who weren't deep in conversation or play, reassuring them that they could sleep in the game room if their tents needed time to dry out, or if they had been blown over in the storm. Then I went over to Mickey and that delicious smelling soup.

"Thank you so much for bringing over some hot food. I hope you didn't get too drenched walking over." I sniffed appreciatively at the big Crock-Pot of soup.

"I came before the rain got too bad," she confessed. "I'd rather be here in a thick cement block building during a storm than my aluminum camper. I do hope it clears up before midnight since I couldn't manage to carry blankets or sleeping gear *and* the Crock-Pot."

I waved a hand. "If you need to curl up and sleep, Lottie has towels by the door. I'm sure you can use them for makeshift bedding." Another flash of lightning followed by a roar of thunder ripped through the air. I held my breath, but the electricity stayed on.

"Do you want some soup?" Mickey asked, already ladling some into a bowl. "It's chicken corn chowder. My own recipe."

I took the bowl, tasted the soup, and made some genuine appreciative noises. "This is amazing," I said after a few bites. "You should sell this."

Her smile was tinged with sadness. "I used to. I got my degree in culinary arts and about ten years ago opened a restaurant in Roanoke. It lasted about five years before I had to throw in the towel and close up shop. I lost everything—all my savings, money my grandparents had left me, everything. It's always a risk opening a business. You probably know that as well, with this campground."

I nodded. "There isn't a day that goes by where I'm not running the numbers and hoping nothing major breaks down."

"It's worse in the food and beverage industry. There are all these licensing hoops you need to jump through, and one complaint, even a wrongful complaint, can cut your business in half overnight." She sighed. "I'm still upset that my dreams were smashed, but what I'm doing now is interesting. And it *is* less time-consuming."

"True." I went to turn away, then thought of something. "I hear there are a lot of problems with inspectors too. Some of them are super nitpicky about things."

She shrugged. "I think every bar and restaurant owner has an inspector complaint. It's not uncommon to get a jerk who insists the temperature of your walk-in is off, even though your reading shows it's just fine."

I made an mmm noise, and left, eating my chowder and thinking.

A woman had called asking for Kendricks's schedule. Mickey had owned a restaurant in the Roanoke area and it had gone under. Had it failed because she'd refused to pay Kendricks blackmail money? Was her place even on Kendricks's route? She did have a history of staying here at the campground, but not always this month. Maybe she'd found out Kendricks had moved to cannabis inspection, read that Danielle had gotten a contract, and timed her stay accordingly. She'd be nearby, and in the month she planned on remaining here, Kendricks was sure to visit Danielle's farm one of those days.

Mickey said she was at the bird sanctuary that day, but she just as easily could have been over at Danielle's killing Kendricks. And the barbeque sauce on the clothes she'd been washing the day after the inspector had been murdered? Maybe it was blood instead.

Should I call Jake? I'd feel like a total idiot if it truly was barbeque sauce on Mickey's clothes, and she surely wasn't the only person with a failed restaurant in Roanoke over the last decade.

By the time I'd finished my soup, I'd decided not to call Jake. There was no sense in dragging him out in the middle of the storm. Besides, even if Mickey was the murderer, I didn't think she'd go on a killing spree in the next twenty-four hours. I'd mention it to Jake tomorrow, just so he could see if her name was on the list of people who had complained about Wilber Kendricks—or even on the list of establishments he inspected over the years.

"What's wrong?" Lottie whispered as I threw my bowl and spoon away. "Is there a leak in the roof? Did Elvis upchuck all those Cheez-Its the kids were feeding him?"

"No, and no," I told her, thankful that my hound had an iron stomach. "I just…this is a stupid idea and I don't want to accuse her or anything, but do you think Mickey might be the person who killed that cannabis inspector?"

"Mickey? The woman with the soup?" Lottie turned to look at the other woman, but did it in a subtle way that I hoped didn't let on we were talking about her. "Why in the world would you think one of your guests is the murderer?"

I stepped closer, keeping my voice low. "Jake said a woman called and asked where Kendricks would be and what his schedule was—claimed she was his daughter. Then there's the necklace I found outside of Danielle's barn. Plus, there evidently had been complaints that Kendricks was on the take—not just his ex-wife either."

Lottie's eyes widened. "Girl, you have been holding back on me! What's this about a necklace? And a woman calling to get Kendricks's schedule?"

"I forgot about the necklace until I saw it when I was doing the wash yesterday," I explained. "Danielle said it wasn't hers and that she'd never seen it before, so I called Jake. I remembered picking it up from the gravel. It wasn't dirty, or bent or broken. It looked like someone had just dropped it."

I pulled up the picture from my phone and showed it to Lottie.

"I've never seen anyone wearing that—at least that I remember," she said. "Although it doesn't look like it's a custom design. I think I've seen that necklace in some of the mall jewelers. It will be hard to trace it back to one particular person."

I pocketed my phone, trying to think if I'd ever seen Mickey wearing a necklace like that. It wasn't the sort of thing a woman would wear hiking or fishing or kayaking. But neither did it seem the kind of accessory a woman would wear to murder someone either.

"So the murderer is a woman," Lottie mused. "She'd called to find out where Kendricks would be. She was wearing this necklace and it fell off when she was taking the murder weapon back to the barn. Right?"

I nodded. "Mickey just told me she used to own a restaurant, but that it went under five years ago. She wasn't at the campground on Tuesday morning—she said she was at the bird sanctuary. And she'd left some clothes in the washer Thursday morning. A guest took them out and put them on the folding table, and when I went to put them in the dryer, I saw they were stained with something red."

"Ooo, I hope you didn't dry them," Lottie said. "That'll set the stain for sure. She'll never get it out."

"I left them on the table for her to rewash," I assured her. "But were those bloodstains on the clothes? Or barbeque sauce as she claimed?"

"And she has poison ivy," Lottie added. "Just like us. She probably got it from walking through those weeds between that dirt road and Danielle's field right after she stashed the inspector's car."

"Other people have poison ivy," I reluctantly pointed out. "At least one other guest complained of it, and I'm sure those weeds aren't the only patch of poison ivy in the area."

"True." Lottie did a quick, side-eye glance at Mickey. "Are you sure about her? Five years seems like a long time to wait for revenge."

"I agree. And I'm sure there are a hundred women who owned or co-owned a restaurant in the Roanoke area or have spilled wine or barbeque sauce on their clothes this week," I added. "I don't think Mickey's a murderer, but I still am going to tell Jake everything so he can at least check her out. Just in case."

Lottie nodded. "Just in case. Because you've had two murderers at your campground. A third doesn't seem too unlikely with that track record."

"Hey." I play-swatted her arm. "Only one guest was a murderer. The other one was the guy from the used book and antiques place. I do not have a track record of harboring murderers."

"Okay, but the campground was involved in both murders," Lottie pointed out. "I'm just saying there might be a connection on this third murder as well."

"The connection is that I found the body," I told her. "Technically Mom found the first body, but I was the one who called it in. So don't go thinking my campground is cursed or anything."

Lottie chuckled. "That means it's you that's cursed. Sassy the Finder of Murder Victims."

As horrible as it was, that did seem to be true.

* * *

THE STORM BLEW out by six o'clock, leaving us with only a persistent light drizzle of rain. We all emerged from the game room like animals descending from Noah's Ark to survey the damage. Most of the tents were collapsed and wet. A few of them had actually been blown like tumbleweeds across the campsite into the woods. It was clear that a good number of my tent campers would be staying in the game room for the night, so Austin, Lottie, and I helped everyone locate their tents and get them set up to dry, moving any of their remaining supplies into the game room. Mom came down with extra towels and bedding from the house, as well as coffee, tea, and hot chocolate for everyone.

Those guests staying in the cabins and in their campers and RVs fared better, but quite a few were walking around the campground to find plastic chairs that had blown away or repairing awnings that had come down in the storm. Elvis and I checked in on everyone while Lottie, Austin, and Mom finished up with the tent campers. Elvis was quivering with excitement over the new smells the rain had unearthed, and managed to sniff out an open packet of hotdogs that was partially underneath an overturned table and eat them all before I noticed.

Satisfied that all my guests were safe and didn't have any serious damages to repair, I took a moment to take stock of the condition of the campground itself.

The buildings had held, thankfully. The kayaks and canoes were still secure in their stands, and the docks and piers were still solid. There was some trash here and there that would need to be picked up, and Austin would have to go around to collect all the sticks and branches that had come down before he mowed next. The only real disaster I could see was the drive leading into the campground.

When Mom and I had returned from the Twelve Gauge, the drive had already been washed out. The gravel had flooded into the grassy areas. The rainwater had taken the path of least resistance and cut huge rivulets into the drive, filling it with a network of long potholes. It would be difficult for people who had lower clearance cars to get in and out, and I worried that anyone trying to get their RV or camper down the drive might suffer undercarriage damage.

This needed to be fixed immediately. First thing in the morning I'd call around and have gravel delivered, then see if someone with a tractor or some type of heavy equipment could come over to spread the gravel and grade the driveway. And unlike the washing machine, this wasn't something I could YouTube-fix myself. I didn't have the gravel, and I didn't have the equipment to handle this project.

"Whew, that storm really took out your drive," Lottie called out from behind me.

I turned to see her speed walking her way toward me, Mom's red rubber boots with big yellow daisies on them adorning her feet.

"This used to happen to us too until Scotty had our drive elevated and blacktopped a few years back," she continued. "Of course, gravel is better when there's ice, but at least we don't have to deal with washouts. Snow removal is easier too."

"How much did it cost you?" I asked, wondering if that was something I could budget for in the future.

"Fifteen grand." Lottie looked around. "If you do the access drives to the cabins and camper sites it would probably run you around thirty."

I shuddered. "Think I'm sticking with gravel for now. Do you know anyone who can get me a load of stone tomorrow? And maybe spread it and level the drive?"

It would save me a whole lot of time calling a dozen

people that my internet search brought up if Lottie could give me a referral.

"Of course! Remember Bart and Bernie? We were talking to them when Squeakers was up on the porch roof? I'm sure they'll be really busy after this storm, but I'll give them a call and tell them you need a load of stone brought by first thing."

"I thought they worked for the county doing road work," I said. "I didn't realize they were contractors."

Lottie nodded. "They're the ones to call if you need stone or have a tree blocking your drive. They did our driveway paving for us. They've got the county roads contract, so that takes precedence over smaller jobs, but I'm sure they can bring some stone out to you since they'll probably be hauling loads of it around tomorrow anyway."

"Thanks. I appreciate it," I told her, wondering who I could call to spread the stone and level the drive. Worst case scenario, Austin and I could fill the deepest of the potholes by hand using the wheelbarrow so at least guests could come and go as they pleased.

"Here comes the cavalry," Lottie said in a joking tone, elbowing me in the side.

I looked up, confused at her words until I saw Jake's truck making its way down my treacherous drive. Lottie and I walked over toward the approaching truck. Jake stopped when he pulled level with us and rolled down his window.

"You all okay here? Thought I'd check in to see if you needed any help."

He looked exhausted, and it made me wonder if he'd been out in the storm doing deputy duties, or busy making sure his horses and property were okay.

"We're all fine." I gestured at the drive. "Just some washout on my road. My tent campers are going to stay in the game room while their equipment dries overnight, but thankfully no one suffered any damage."

"How about you, Lottie?" he asked.

She shrugged. "I haven't been home yet, but I'm sure my place is fine. The house is up on high ground, and the driveway never floods. I might find my patio furniture across the lawn, but that's probably it."

"That's good to hear." He sighed. "Brock Yelts down the road had a tree come down on his house, and Nan Swinton's sump pump failed. She had about a foot of water backed up into her basement. I'm just coming back from loaning her my spare pump."

"Does Brock need a place to stay?" Lottie asked. "He's welcome at my place."

Jake shook his head. "He's good. We put up some tarps and I dropped him off at the Community Center in town. They're organizing offers of spare rooms and guest houses for people whose houses were damaged."

I hadn't realized how bad the storm had been. Hearing about my neighbors made me doubly grateful that I only had a rutted driveway to deal with.

"Before you go, Sassy has more information to tell you about the Kendricks murder case," Lottie said to Jake.

It took me a second to remember. Dealing with the storm and my guests had pushed my suspicions of Mickey right out of my mind.

"It's a whole lot of circumstantial stuff," I told Jake, embarrassed that I was even mentioning this to him. "You said you all were suspecting the killer was a woman because of the calls trying to get information on Kendricks's schedule, and then there was the necklace I found. Well, I was talking to one of my guests today and she said about five years ago she owned a restaurant in Roanoke that had gone under."

"Up to ninety percent of restaurants fail in their first year," Jake said. "A third don't make it past five years. Having owned a failed restaurant isn't enough to make someone a suspect."

I flushed at his gentle tone, feeling like a total fool. "I know, but she was off-site the day of the murder. I remember she said she was at the bird sanctuary, but maybe she was lying about that."

"And there was the clothes," Lottie chimed in. "Tell him about the clothes."

I nodded. "Thursday morning someone had washed clothes and left them in the machine. Another guest took them out and put them on the changing table. When I went to dry them, I noticed they had red stains on them. Mickey admitted they were hers, that she'd gotten busy with a work call and forgotten to put them in the dryer. She said the stains were barbeque sauce, but what if they weren't?"

It sounded ridiculous, and I was mortified for wasting Jake's time like this.

"It's a stretch," Jake said. "But I'll check her name against the list of restaurants Kendricks covered and those who complained about him. I'll run by the bird sanctuary to check out her alibi as well."

It was kind of him to humor me like this, especially since I knew he had a million things to do and chasing down long-shot leads shouldn't take precedence over those other things.

"If you don't think it's relevant, then you don't have to check into it," I told him. "I just thought you should know in case she was a suspect for some reason. Otherwise, don't worry about it."

"It's worth a quick call to the bird sanctuary," he assured me, picking up a pad of paper and a pen from the center console. "What's her name?"

"Mickey Marx." I described her, thinking the people at the bird sanctuary might not have registered her name. Heck, they might not remember her at all.

Jake wrote the information down, then put the pad and pen aside. "If you ladies are doing okay, I'm going to head on down the road to check in on some of our other neighbors."

Lottie and I waved him off, then headed back to the house. "I feel like a suspicious old lady," I confessed. "One of those nosy women who spies on her neighbors out the window and gossips about them to the whole community."

"No, that's me," Lottie laughed, tucking my arm through hers. "The killer might not be Mickey, but if it is, then that information could help the police narrow their search down and maybe even get a warrant."

"That's true," I replied, thinking that sometimes it was better to have more information than none at all.

CHAPTER 22

I'd offered Austin a spot on my couch for the night, but he insisted he'd have no problems making it home. Normally I wouldn't doubt the capabilities of my young helper to drive home at nine at night, but I wasn't sure what the road conditions were like, so I made him call his parents and alert them that he was on his way. I also made him promise that if he encountered any road closures or significant detours, that he'd come back to stay here.

Lottie cheerfully announced that she was sure she could make the short drive next door, and that, no offense, her bed was probably a lot more comfortable than my couch. I winced while her BMW navigated the ruins of my drive, before heading back inside.

Mom and I stayed up in case anyone needed us, but things at the campground were quiet. The lights over at the game room stayed on until ten o'clock. After that I saw the occasional bobbing dot of light in the room, or moving out across the grounds to the bathrooms. Mom went to bed soon after, but I couldn't sleep, so Elvis and I stayed up, watching old reruns and finishing off a bag of chips.

The next morning I overslept, and was jolted awake at six by an enormous crashing noise. In a panic, I jumped out of bed, my tangled bedsheets almost causing me to fall flat on the floor. All sorts of disaster scenarios raced through my mind as I ran through the living room to the door. Someone's RV exploding. Someone driving into the side of a building. A tree falling onto a cabin or someone's camper.

Fearing the worst, I flung open the door and instead saw a dump truck banging out the last bit of stone into a huge pile beside the garage.

Bart waved at me from the driver's seat. "Nice pajamas," he shouted.

They were nice, mainly because they had giant yellow daisies all over them.

"Thanks," I shouted back. It was six in the morning and it probably wasn't polite for either of us to be shouting, but if the truck and the avalanche of stone hadn't woken every one of my guests, then our voices certainly wouldn't. Normally, I'd be in a panic about the early morning noise, but I was grateful for the stone delivery no matter the hour. And although my guests might not appreciate the rude awakening, they certainly would appreciate being able to navigate my driveway without losing a muffler.

I snapped on Elvis's leash, slipped on my flip flops, and with my daisy pajamas walked over to Bart. "What do I owe you?" I said, still shouting because the truck was just as noisy here as it was twenty feet away in my house.

"I'll invoice you," he replied.

The dump portion of the truck snapped back into place and a few seconds later, Bernie hopped into the passenger seat. We waved, then Elvis and I stood back as the men bounced the huge dump truck down my rutted drive and out to their next job.

I had stone, but it was still going to be a long day's work

for Austin and me to wheelbarrow it back and forth, filling in all these potholes. I planned on making some calls this morning, but doubted I'd be able to get someone out today to grade the driveway. I probably would have been lower on Bart and Bernie's delivery list if Lottie hadn't phoned them last night and called in a favor—one more reason I owed her big-time.

Mom was awake when Elvis and I returned to the house —no surprise there. I was pretty sure everyone in my camp-ground was awake now. She offered to take care of Elvis, leaving me to throw on some clothes, run over to the camp store, and hurriedly get the coffee urns going. I wasn't the only one running late today. Flora and the food delivery van didn't get in until seven o'clock and she let me know there were several road closures in Reckless with downed trees and fallen powerlines blocking them.

The news made me worry for Austin, but I was sure either he or his parents would have called if something had happened. Even so, I was happy to see his truck coming down the drive at noon. What surprised me was the vehicle following him—a flatbed truck with some kind of backhoe on top.

Austin pulled into the lot, but the flatbed drove around to the garage and parked. A woman with her dark curly hair held back with a blue bandana hopped out of the cab, her crimson lips curling into a smile when she saw me coming toward her.

"Danielle, what are you doing here? Is this yours?" I gestured toward the thing on the bed of the truck. It had a wide shovel-like scoop in the front, and a digging bucket at the end of a jointed arm in the rear. Was it a backhoe? A loader? It was definitely some kind of construction equipment.

"Nope. This beauty belongs to Tony Hershbaugh over at

Four Seasons Equipment Rentals. I've got to have it back by two, so I don't have much time to chat. That driveway of yours isn't going to fix itself, you know? I won't say no to a cup of coffee, though. I haven't had my quota of caffeine yet, and it's going to be a long day."

I stared at her, completely confused. "You rented a backhoe? And drove it here? To fix my driveway?"

"I'm just the labor," she told me. "Jake called in a favor from Tony, so technically no one rented the backhoe. But I did drive it here, and I'm fixing your driveway—as soon as I get some coffee, that is."

"Cream? Sugar?" I asked, not about to delay further in getting Danielle her caffeine.

"Nope. Black with no sugar, the way God intended coffee to be." With a cheerful grin, she walked around the side of the truck and began unhooking the backhoe.

By the time I came back with her coffee, she was up in the cab, driving the monstrous thing off the flatbed. I handed it up to her, then stood back to watch as she skillfully maneuvered the backhoe to the pile of stone, scooping up a load and heading down toward the front of the drive.

I was speechless, overwhelmed with gratitude. It hadn't been two full months since I'd bought this campground and arrived here in Reckless, and already I had friends who'd shown me such kindness. Lottie had gotten me the stone delivery first thing this morning. Jake had arranged for equipment to spread the stone and grade my driveway. And Danielle—who I'd just met not even a week ago—was here doing the work.

It was wonderful to have such good friends. If this wasn't some sort of sign that buying the campground was the right thing to do, then I didn't know what was.

Thank you for the backhoe, I texted Jake as I headed back to the camp store.

No problem, his reply said. *Wanted to tell you that Mickey's alibi checked out. And the restaurant she owned wasn't one that Kendricks inspected.* A second text added.

So sorry I sent you on a wild goose chase with that. My crazy imagination, I replied.

I was relieved that Mickey wasn't the killer, but it was a little embarrassing that I'd wasted Jake's time with my paranoia.

The rest of my afternoon was spent with helping the dislocated campers move back into their tents, cleaning up the game room after its overnight occupancy, and admiring the amazing job Danielle did in leveling and spreading gravel on my drive.

Around four I decided to take a break, so I hung the "be back later" sign on the door and went down to sit on the dock with a book. As I made my way across the sun-warmed boards, I saw that I wasn't the only one with that idea—Bree sat on the edge of the dock, her bare feet dangling in the water and a book by her side. Her face was lifted toward the sun, the rays reflecting off the mirror of her sunglasses.

She patted the spot beside her. "Come join me, Sassy," she offered. "It's such a beautiful day after that storm last night. It always amazes me how nature can blow through with such violence, then the next day be all warm sunshine and light."

"What are you reading?" I asked as I settled into a spot beside her on the dock and began to take off my shoes and socks.

She held up the paperback. "*That First Dance.* It's a romance. High school teacher and the new football coach."

"Let me guess, she's the teacher and he's the coach?" I guessed. "Although it would be really interesting to have a romance where the woman was the sports coach and the man was the straightlaced history teacher nearly failing her star player. They'd work together to help the kid pass, stay on the team, and get that college scholarship he so desperately needed."

"That's pretty much the story, except he's the coach and she's a math teacher." Bree sighed. "I love a geek-jock romance. And I love an enemies-to-lovers romance too, but not when they're mean or anything. In this book, she's mad because she thinks he's trying to get her to just pass his player even though he's failing, and he's mad because he thinks she doesn't care about the sports kid's potential college scholarship. They have it out at the homecoming dance, only to find that the kids had voted for them to have the first teacher dance together."

"And sparks fly?" I grinned, because I loved this kind of story.

"Sparks were flying before the dance, but the gym decorations were ready to ignite after." She pushed the book over to me. "I just finished it, so if you want to read it, go ahead."

"I'm not sure I can get it done before you all leave on Thursday," I warned, thinking of my schedule.

She shrugged. "Then keep it. I've got three more books in my suitcase I haven't even read yet."

I thanked her and grabbed the book, thinking it sounded a whole lot more fun than the one on the Decline of the American Chestnut I'd grabbed off the shelf next to my fireplace.

"I hope you all got through the storm okay," I said after I'd tucked the book into my bag.

"Snug as bugs in a rug," Bree announced. "We had Courtney and Caleb over at our cabin and we all sat around playing cards and eating chips. I was a little worried when the lights flickered that one time, but we were ready with flashlights and extra batteries."

"Oh good. We had most of the tent campers in the game

room through this morning, but everyone was in good spirits."

She grimaced. "I would have hated to have been in a tent last night. It's a good thing you had shelter for them."

"Any big plans for the rest of your vacation?" I asked.

"Hiking, fishing, and some kayaking. I think we might do another picnic on that island with Courtney and Caleb. I really just want to take it easy for the rest of the trip." She shifted, turning to face me. "Hey, you wouldn't happen to have a metal detector I can rent or borrow, would you?"

"No, but you might be able to pick up one in Derwood," I told her. "Are you planning on going to one of the battle-fields? I think they have some restrictions on using metal detectors there, so you might want to call ahead before you go buy one."

"I was actually just going to use it around the camp-ground to find a lost necklace. I'd probably never use it again, so I didn't actually want to buy a metal detector."

My heart raced at her words, but I quickly doused my excitement. People lost necklaces all the time. I had a lost and found box in the camp store full of stuff people left behind or lost while they were here. Just as Mickey owning a restaurant that failed and having red-stains on some clothes didn't make her a murderer, Bree losing a necklace didn't make her one either.

"Can you describe it?" I asked her. "When and where do you think you lost it? People turn stuff in all the time. I'll keep an eye open for it and go through our lost and found box to see if someone brought it by the store."

"It's a gold chain with a gold heart pendant that has some diamond chips down one side of the heart. Courtney's brother gave it to her for her birthday a few months before he died. I noticed she wasn't wearing it Tuesday night, but didn't say anything because I thought maybe that was a symbol of her processing her grief, but Caleb asked her about it last night and she said she lost it." Bree shook her head. "She said it was no big deal, but I'm sure it hurt her terribly to lose a memento like that. I was thinking I could take a metal detector around the parking area and maybe I could find it. Although she probably lost it when she was shopping in town."

My excitement was back. "Would you recognize the necklace if you saw it?"

She nodded. "I think so. It wasn't really unusual, but I remember what it looked like."

I pulled out my phone and opened the picture I'd taken in the laundry room, turning the screen to Bree.

"That's it," she squealed. "I can't believe you actually found it! Where was it?"

"At a farm where a man was murdered on Tuesday," I told her.

Bree frowned in confusion. "I don't understand. Maybe it's not her necklace after all. I mean, I can't imagine what Courtney would be doing at a farm, unless there was a craft show there or something. She was shopping Tuesday in town. And what's this about a murder?"

Maybe it wasn't Courtney's necklace after all. I'd jumped to conclusions about Mickey and didn't want to do the same here. It wasn't all that unusual of a jewelry design, after all. Although it might seem a crazy coincidence that two women lost very similar necklaces in roughly the same town on roughly the same day, it wasn't beyond the realm of statistical possibility.

"Was she wearing the necklace Tuesday morning?" I tried to remember if she'd had it on when she'd come in for coffee, or if she'd been wearing it when the four were in the camp store talking about the horseback riding expedition late that afternoon. If she'd had it on then, she couldn't have been the murderer, since I'd already had the necklace I'd found in my pocket from the crime scene.

"I'm not sure. I know she had it on Monday night because we went for a late-night dip in the lake, and I remember the gold and diamonds sparkling in the moonlight, and thinking I wouldn't want to risk losing something so sentimental swimming in a lake at night. Maybe she lost it then?" Bree frowned. "No, I remember seeing it on her when we were toweling off. I think she lost it sometime Tuesday or early Wednesday, because when we all went fishing on Wednesday morning, I noticed she didn't have it on."

That narrowed the coincidence considerably.

"If she lost it Tuesday, then why didn't she raise the alarm then?" I asked. "If I'd lost something so important and senti-mental, I'd be asking neighboring campers, searching the cabin, going through the lost and found box. I'd be frantic."

"I know. It is kinda weird," Bree confessed. "When Caleb asked her about it last night, she just shrugged and said it might be tangled in her dirty clothes or in her luggage, and that it would probably turn up when they were packing. I wouldn't be so nonchalant about something like that. And honestly, she *did* look upset about it even though she said she wasn't. Maybe she was embarrassed and didn't want to cause a fuss?"

Maybe. But if I'd lost the last gift my brother had given me, *I'd* sure be causing a fuss.

"But what's this about a murder? You said someone was murdered on a farm?" Bree asked again.

"An inspector," I said, still thinking about the necklace. "He was inspecting a farm growing cannabis under contract to the state."

I winced at Bree's horrified expression, wishing I'd kept my mouth shut about the murder.

"The police believe the murder was personal. This wasn't

a random killing or anything," I said, trying to think of some way to convince Bree that she and the other campers were safe, and that this wasn't the start of a slasher horror movie.

"Still. That's horrible." She bit her lip. "Although people get murdered in the city all the time. I guess it isn't so weird that someone would get killed out in the country like this. It just never crossed my mind that someone might be murdered where I was on vacation."

"The farm is on the other side of Reckless, far away from the campground. This didn't have anything to do with the campground, or the town. It's very safe here," I told her, completely ignoring the fact that this was the third murder that had taken place in the area within the last two months, and that the other two murders *had* taken place right here at the campground. Good grief. Maybe this *was* the start of a slasher horror movie.

She nodded, not looking quite convinced. "It's kind of creepy, though."

I needed to switch the conversation or I'd find that Drew and Bree along with a number of other campers were packing up to leave due to a local murder.

"I'll keep an eye open for Courtney's necklace. Hopefully it's in her cabin somewhere, but just in case I'll spread the word and ask other campers if they've seen it."

Hopping up, I thanked Bree again for the book and walked back to the store, mulling over our conversation. Should I call Jake? I hated to bother him about what was probably another set of coincidences. He was busy enough without my wasting his time, making him run down leads that went to nowhere. One not-so-unusual necklace wasn't enough to accuse a woman of murder.

Still, it bothered me enough that when I got to the house, I told Mom the whole story, thinking it would be good to get her take on the situation and let her weigh in on what I should do.

"What would Courtney's motive be?" Mom asked when I'd finished the tale.

"Well, it can't be self-defense, because no one goes into another person's barn and picks up a tamping rod just in case they get attacked while trespassing on a farm," I pointed out. "Jake said a woman called asking for Kendricks's schedule, so if Courtney *did* murder the inspector, there had to have been something personal between them."

"You'd thought maybe the killer was someone Kendricks was blackmailing, a bar or restaurant owner he was hitting up for money. Did Courtney own a restaurant that went under? Or maybe her husband, Caleb, did?"

"Or maybe her brother," I mused. "He died recently, possibly by suicide, and Courtney has been hit hard by his death. She might have held Kendricks responsible."

"That sounds like a good motive, but we don't know anything about her brother," Mom pointed out. "Courtney is using her married name, so it's not like we could look up restaurant listings, or closings or articles in the paper."

"True. And I don't feel right going to Jake about this without more proof—not after I had him running around checking Mickey's alibi and cross checking her name against the places Kendricks inspected."

Mom tapped her chin a few times before speaking. "I could probably pull up all the obituaries for Roanoke County in the last few months, and download the ones within an appropriate age range. Then I can search the survived-by names for Courtney's. Once I get her brother's name, I can look to see if he had any business licenses, and if there was any mention of his business in the paper. If he had a restaurant that closed, and his grieving sister lost a necklace just like the one you found at the crime scene, then would you feel better about going to Jake with this?"

I would, but it felt so intrusive. I hated the thought of us digging through obituaries to pry into the circumstances of a guest's brother's tragic death. And so what if he *had* owned a restaurant or bar and it had gone under? As Jake said, lots of people had failed businesses. I felt bad enough for thinking Mickey was a killer, I'd feel horrible pointing the police toward a grieving sister.

"No, I don't want to do that," I finally told Mom. "Let's just leave it be. I'll text Jake about my conversation with Bree, and if I look like a paranoid fool, then so be it. But other than that, I think I need to just let the police handle this one, and focus on my guests and the campground."

"Okay." Mom's smile was reassuring. "I'll put the word out about Courtney's missing necklace, and I'll go through the lost-and-found box."

"No, I will do that," I told her. "Because this is your day off. Elvis and I will head back over to the camp store while you relax."

Mom waved her hand. "I had enough relaxing at my knitting club already. But you're right. Maybe I'll sit on the porch with some iced tea and read."

It was a great idea—one I intended on using when my day off came around. And speaking of reading...

"I've got the perfect book for you," I said, handing her the romance Bree had given me. "Enjoy. And don't spoil the ending for me."

CHAPTER 23

I sent Jake a quick text about my conversation with Bree and had mixed feelings when he didn't respond. Maybe he was annoyed with my meddling. Hopefully he was just busy and realized a guest losing a necklace similar to the one I'd found wasn't a priority. Deciding that I'd done my civic duty, I stuck my phone back into my pocket and got to work restocking the store.

Sunday was typically a slow day, and after yesterday's weather, pretty much every guest in the campground was off enjoying the day. Every canoe and kayak was rented out until this evening. People were out on the trails, out on the lake, or lying about the beach, or the docks. When I went out to sweep the porch, I smelled the distinctive aroma of charcoal on grills, and glanced at my watch, realizing it was almost dinnertime.

Elvis stood up from his spot on the porch, shaking off the dust and sniffing the air.

"Burgers? Or steaks?" I asked him. "Or is it both that someone's cooking tonight?"

He sneezed then sniffed again, a long line of drool hanging from his lip.

"Either one smells pretty good, doesn't it?" My stomach growled, confirming that the thought of steak or hamburger appealed to me as well.

I unhooked the hound's leash and scooted his water bowl over to the side. "Come on inside. It's not steak, but I've got some dog treats under the counter. Want a treat? Treat?"

Elvis's ears came forward at the familiar word, his droopy eyes fixed intently on my face. I opened the door and he trotted in ahead of me, his nails clicking on the hardwood. He headed around the counter and nosed the bag on the shelf behind the counter, knowing right where the snacks were. I bent down and dug a couple of them out, putting the bag back before feeding them to the eager hound.

When I stood, I was surprised to see Courtney standing at the counter.

"Oh sheesh." My hand went to my chest. "You startled me."

"Sorry." She shifted her weight from foot to foot, her gaze dropping to the counter. "Bree talked to me. She said you were going to look in the lost and found for my necklace and put out some fliers, but I wanted to tell you not to bother because I found it."

"You did?" Now I was *really* embarrassed that I'd texted Jake.

"Bree told me about someone dying...being murdered at a farm, and that you'd found a necklace there that looked like mine. She thought maybe someone had stolen it—that the killer had stolen it, and it fell out of his pocket by the barn."

I'd never mentioned that I'd found the necklace by the barn.

"So you and Bree looked for the necklace in your cabin and found it?" I asked. "Why aren't you wearing it now?"

Her hand went to her neck. "No. I found it earlier. The clasp was broken, so I'm not wearing it. I'll need to get it fixed first."

"So you found it this morning?" I waited for her nod. "Why don't I run you in to town to get it fixed? I know how important the necklace is—Bree told me that your brother gave it to you. I'm sure you'll want to get it fixed right away. I'm surprised you didn't say anything when it went missing... on Tuesday, right?"

"I was sure it was in the cabin somewhere," she said. "And I'll wait until I get home to get it fixed. I'd rather take it to a local jeweler—no offense to any jewelers in Reckless."

"I understand." I watched her carefully, her shaking hands, her gaze darting around the store. "It's a pretty necklace. So strange that yours went missing the exact same day the exact same piece of jewelry winds up a clue at a murder scene."

She sucked in a breath but didn't respond.

"I turned that necklace in to the police. It probably has fingerprints on it and DNA. Just like the murder weapon that someone didn't wipe down as carefully as they thought they did. Just like the car that someone ditched in the woods behind the field. I'm sure that person got a nasty case of poison ivy going through those weeds, too." I waited a few seconds to let that sink in. "I'm sure that person had a good reason for wanting the inspector dead. There'd been complaints about him, that he was blackmailing bar and restaurant owners, that he was squeezing them for payoffs, saying he'd write up their businesses and get them shut down if they didn't pay him. He'd allegedly been doing this for decades, ruining people's lives, and no one did anything about it. He sounds like he was a horrible man."

Courtney's breath choked on a sob and she finally looked up at me, her face wet with tears. "I didn't mean to. I just

217

wanted to face him, to tell him what he did. My brother died because of him. That pub meant everything to David. He filed a complaint, and no one cared. His business went under and no one cared. When he died…I cared. I wanted that man to know what he'd done, just to tell him face-to-face."

"And he didn't care," I said softly.

Her hands clenched into fists. "He said he didn't know who David was and didn't care. He laughed at me. I went to leave, and saw the barn with all the tools. I just thought I'd hit him once, but I couldn't stop. And when I realized what I'd done, I panicked. I put the metal pole back in the barn. His keys were in his car, so I moved it down off the side of some dirt road, then ran as fast as I could through the field to my car and came straight back here." She shook her head. "I showered and changed and hid my clothes before anyone saw me. When Caleb and Drew and Bree got back from their hike, I was sitting on the cabin porch, reading. They don't know. None of them knew."

The door to the camp store opened. Jake walked in, followed by Sean. From their grim expressions, I realized they didn't need to hear her confession. They knew.

"You have to tell the police, Courtney," I told her. "They'll find out."

"We've already found out," Jake said. "The data from the phone company came in this morning. The two calls that came in asking about William Kendricks's work schedule were from your cell phone and the location ping showed the call originated here at the campground. There's a record of your brother's complaint to the state alcohol board about Kendricks. And the necklace found at the scene matches one you were seen wearing up until Tuesday. That's enough for a warrant to search your cabin and vehicle for other evidence. And it's enough to compare your fingerprints and DNA against that found on the murder weapon and the victim's car."

With that, Sean read Courtney her rights while Jake cuffed her. The pair led her out to the waiting police cruiser, while I watched with a whole lot of conflicted feelings.

CHAPTER 24

"*I* really feel sorry for her," Lottie said. "The woman was grieving. Kendricks was a total jerk, and was a criminal. She snapped."

Lottie, Mom, and I were sitting on the camp store porch drinking tea and watching the sun set. Elvis snoozed at our feet. Everything was peaceful—at the moment, anyway.

Courtney was being held at the police station on murder charges. Caleb had paced back and forth in front of their cabin as the police searched it, on the phone trying to find a lawyer for his wife. Drew and Bree had stood awkwardly nearby, clearly horrified over the happenings, and trying to do their best to reassure Caleb that everything would be okay.

Everything would not be okay—not for Courtney and Caleb.

Kendricks was a horrible man, but he didn't deserve to be murdered. He deserved to be fired and sent to jail for his crimes, but not murdered. But I still couldn't blame Courtney for what she'd done. Part of me wished I'd never found that necklace, never poked my nose into this investigation.

None of that would have mattered in the end. The police still would have traced the call from her cell phone. They would have made the connection between her brother and Kendricks. They would have matched her prints to those at the scene. But no matter how many times I told myself this, I still felt guilty. I liked Courtney. I liked her husband, and Drew and Bree, and I wished none of this had ever happened.

"I think the liquor board bears a lot of the blame in this." Mom reached out to pat my shoulder. "They had multiple complaints against Kendricks. There should have been more of an investigation. They should have looked into his finances, maybe interviewed other bar and restaurant owners. The fact that he was able to run this scam of his for decades is shameful. He hurt a lot of people and their businesses."

I nodded. "I hope she gets a good lawyer. I hope they put Kendricks's ex-wife, and all the businesses he stole from on the stand at her trial."

"If it even goes to court." Lottie snorted. "I doubt the county or the state wants their dirty laundry aired all over. I hope there's a decent plea deal for her."

"I almost wish Dean's friend Bulldog had taken care of Kendricks instead," Mom said. "Then maybe Courtney's brother would still be alive and she wouldn't be in jail."

It was a horrible thing to say, but I kind of agreed. We sat for a while, drinking our tea and watching as the sun vanished and lights all around the campground twinkled to life. It was hard to stay sad while looking at such beauty.

A few guests walked by with flashlights in hand. They waved, greeted us, then continued on, laughing as they spoke.

"I need some good news," I said, downing the rest of my tea.

"Bookings are solid for next week," Mom announced.

"MarySue Bowman won the stick-horse race down Main Street for the third year running," Lottie said.

"That book you lent me today was really good," Mom added.

"Squeakers escaped again, this time out a basement window, and made it to the Bait and Beer with enough time to win fifty dollars at poker before Celeste came to take him home," Lottie told us.

I laughed at that.

"What's your good news?" Mom asked me.

I reached down to scratch Elvis's ear. "I have a new friend —Danielle. And I'm so happy to have you, Mom, and Sierra, and Lottie, and Jake in my life. And this hound dog here."

And the best news of all? I was alive. I'd beaten cancer, and was here enjoying a beautiful evening at the campground I'd adored as a child, surrounded by the people and dog I loved.

I was living the dream. And the occasional storm, the occasional moment of tragedy, wasn't going to overshadow that piece of good news.

* * *

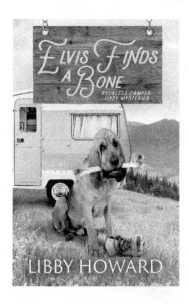

PREORDER the next nook in the Reckless Camper Cozy Mystery Series is Elvis Finds a Bone!

CAN'T WAIT THAT LONG? Try my other books in the Locust Point Mystery Series, starting with The Tell All.

NEVER MISS a new release or a sale. Sign up for my newsletter and get all the fun with none of the spam.

ALSO BY LIBBY HOWARD

Locust Point Mystery Series:

The Tell All

Junkyard Man

Antique Secrets

Hometown Hero

A Literary Scandal

Root of All Evil

A Grave Situation

Last Supper

A Midnight Clear

Fire and Ice

Best In Breed

Cold Waters

Five for a Dollar

Lonely Hearts - coming in 2022

Reckless Camper Mystery Series -

The Handyman Homicide

Death is on the Menu

The Green Rush

Elvis Finds a Bone

ACKNOWLEDGMENTS

Special thanks to Lyndsey Lewellen for cover design and Kimberly Cannon for editing.

In memory of my mother who was my biggest fan and my partner-in-crime.

ABOUT THE AUTHOR

Libby Howard lives in a little house in the woods with her sons and two exuberant bloodhounds. She occasionally knits, occasionally bakes, and occasionally manages to do a load of laundry. Most of her writing is done in a bar where she can combine work with people-watching, a decent micro-brew, and a plate of Old Bay wings.

For more information:
libbyhowardbooks.com/

9 781952 216602